THOMAS STACEY

1861-D

outskirts
press

For
Sandra
and
for all the
Chrissy's of the world

To

*My sisters in law Mary Lou and Elyse who have
supported me in so many ways over the last few years.
Thank You ladies!*

Special thanks to my editors
My grandniece Kaitlyn
My son Craig
My daughter in law Nora

Other books by Thomas Stacey
The Sam Browne
Alone, Together, Nevermore
Massacre of the Innocents

PROLOGUE

He travelled alone and mostly by night. He wanted to avoid any danger he possibly could, as he made his way northward. It had been almost a month since he was paroled from his duty in the Confederate Army. Most of all the other soldiers he served with on the gold treasure assignment made their way to their homes in the South. He was heading back to Michigan – where he came from originally. He hated the cold Michigan winters where he had lived with his sister and her husband and two children. His plan was to head south, find work, save up and buy a small farm and enjoy the warm southern climate. The Civil War got in the way of his plans. He had just taken up residence in the South as the war broke out. The draft came quickly and he was conscripted into the Confederate States of America (CSA) Army. He didn't have strong feelings either way as far as the political reasons for the war. Slavery was just a take it or leave it as far as he was concerned. He knew that if he returned to Michigan, he would be drafted into the Union Army . . . so why not stay where it's warm? He was among the lucky ones – if you could call it that. For four years he was living off the land and fighting mostly to stay alive with the occasional field battle. He didn't sustain any physical injuries – only the mental ones – the atrocities of war!

His luck turned at the end of the war – April 1865. One of his last assignments was to guard the Confederate gold that was being moved from Charlotte, North Carolina. The goal was to move the gold further south – possibly Georgia. Ships and bridges were burned to prevent the Yankees from using the ships and to slow their pursuit of the CSA gold treasure. It was a haphazard journey as the gold moved from city to city, on trains to wagons and then back to trains, often switching command and guards along the way. Near Abbeville, South Carolina the entire gold treasure was transferred from railroad boxcars onto horse-drawn wagons to be transported to Washington, Georgia. After the gold was loaded on the wagons and they started their journey south, his commander ordered him to go back and check all the boxcars to insure they were all empty. He did as he was ordered. As he entered the last car, he felt he may as well empty his bladder in the privacy of the empty boxcar. He went to one of the corners, unbuttoned his fly and was about to start, when he tripped on something pushed into the corner. It was a small wooden box covered with a piece of burlap. He removed the burlap. The top of the ammo-style box was imprinted with the acronym *CSA*, a Confederate flag and the words *Dahlonega Mint*. He opened the box and his mouth fell agape as he saw the shiny gold coins filling the box. All the weeks that the troops had been guarding the gold, none of the soldiers or midshipmen from the ships had actually seen the specie or even the paper money. It was all hidden in iron chests, wooden boxes and saddlebags. With all the excitement of what he had just found, he almost forgot why entered the boxcar; he walked over to the opposite corner and proceeded to empty his bladder and he thought excitedly, about what he had just uncovered. He quickly decided to take a little for himself and turn the rest over to General Basil Duke, his commander. He reasoned that turning in the box of gold would take away any suspicion. The transferring of the gold back and forth from boxcars to wagons and back to boxcars was so disorganized that no one knew for sure what may have been taken, lost or misplaced throughout the grueling trek. He scooped out two handfuls of the gold dollars and brought them up to his face. He could smell the metal and dream about what it could do for his uncertain future. He stuffed handfuls of gold dollars into the bottom of his haversack, covered it with his meager supplies and slung it over his shoulder. No time to count now! The remaining gold in the box was too heavy to carry back to the rest of the unit so he hopped off the boxcar and hailed another soldier nearby to help him carry the box back to the wagons.

He had been on the road for some time. He lost track of time. Days and nights merged into one another. He just knew the physical exertion was taking its toll. The further he walked the heavier the haversack got on his back. His food supply was running low and he needed rest. If he hadn't been in such a dire physical and mental state, he would have appreciated the beautiful vista that drifted into sight as he reached the top of a small hill. A full moon lit up waves of sparkling diamonds, on the surface of a large lake. He felt that this would be a good spot to take an extended rest, take inventory of his meager supplies and try to get some of his strength back and plan for what was yet to come. As he swept his eyes across the lake, he noticed a small island close to shore on the opposite side of the lake. He thought that this would be a good place to take refuge if he could find a way to get there and if it didn't show any signs of human life.

As he got closer to the island, he saw what appeared to be a sandbar extending from the island and tapering off toward the shoreline. *Don't need a boat*, he thought. He decided to remove his brogans and raggedy socks, roll up his pant legs and wade over to the island. He hadn't washed his socks or clothes since he started and the ripeness was overwhelming him as he thought about it. He tied his boots together and slung them over his shoulder and gingerly took his first step into the sand – careful to make sure he was on a solid footing– and not on quicksand. The shock of the cold water quickly wore off and transformed into a refreshing coolness that wandered up his weary legs. The sandbar to the island was about 25 yards and he enjoyed every step in the cool sandy bottom.

When he reached the island, he found a sizeable log close to shore and he rolled it next to the water and sat down and took a deep breath. He dipped the socks repeatedly in the water wrung them out and repeated the process until he was sure the socks were at least moderately clean. A thought came to mind as he draped the socks over the log to dry. He undid his belt – with the brass CSA insignia buckle, undid the buttons on his pants, removed them and his long-legged drawers and proceeded to give his disgusting underwear the same treatment as his socks. He put his pants back on, spread out his bedroll, leaned his head on the log and waited for his socks and drawers to dry.

A few hours into his much-needed sleep an insect landing on his nose awoke him from a light slumber. It was still dark out, but the moon scattered some light onto the shore as he felt for his socks. They were still damp. He decided he needed to see what else was on the island. He wanted to be safe and get away from the shoreline and out of sight. He put on his brogans, sans socks and gathered his drawers, bedroll and haversack – which seemed to have gotten lighter – as he made his way inland. The island was close to twenty five acres. The lake, he estimated unconsciously, was about ten times that size. Close to where he landed was what appeared to be a foot-trail at one time. The brush was tamped down, but still had some growth sticking up, leading him to believe that there wasn't any recent traffic. The moon was waning on the horizon, but there was still enough visibility with his night-sight to make out where he was going. After an hour or so, of feeling his way through the path that occasionally disappeared, he spotted the silhouette of a structure against the blue-gray lightening sky. Not knowing what it was, he approached it cautiously. It was a small log cabin with a fieldstone chimney on one side. He didn't see any movement or light coming from the cabin, so he approached closer, and as he did, he noticed that most of the perimeter was inundated with huge amounts of wild buckthorn, weeds and sapling

VI

trees. Even the doorway was covered with a thick red ivy vine crawling up the door and encircling the door jamb. This was a good sign he thought . . . no signs of recent occupancy.

Still keeping his cautionary hat on, he walked up to the door and slowly pushed on it. It resisted at first, squeaked lightly, and then smoothly opened into the one-room interior. The one glassless window on the moon-side of the cabin gave him just enough light to survey the surroundings. There was a mixture of smells from: the log-oak walls, the dirt-floor, musty leaves gathered in the corners, damp partially burned logs in the fireplace and he was sure that more than one critter had died there recently. The furnishings were meager. There was a wooden table and two wooden chairs. Both were cobbled out of roughhewn lumber, probably left over from the cutting of the log walls. The fireplace with the partially burned logs had a metal cooking pot on the hearth. The cabin floor was packed dirt that absorbed most of the smells and then released them with the slightest disturbance or move-ment of the air. He felt somewhat secure and sat down cautiously on one of the chairs. *A fire would be nice*, he thought but decided against it . . . but then, on second thought, he was going to chance it. He took a mental inventory of the half-burned wood in the fireplace and some kindling in one of the corners. He went outside and found some arm length dried-out branches, small enough that he could stomp on them and break them to fit in the fireplace. Luckily, he had a piece of dry flint and a pocket knife. He gathered some kindling, a bird's nest from one of the rafters and a handful of dried leaves. After a few tries of striking the flint with his knife, he was successful in igniting the tinder. Persistent blowing - enough to make him dizzy – paid off when the embers erupted into soul-warming fire.

Once he got the fire going, he felt a profound sense of relief. He felt that he was getting close to his destination in Michigan where he could contact his sister and finally settle down. The gold heft in his haversack added to the feeling of security. He sat down at the table and put on his socks and drawers which were still warm from drying near the fire. He opened the haversack and decided to take a count. There was: the gold specie at the bottom, his shot bag where he kept his food supply now consisting of a few pieces of beef jerky, three pieces of hardtack, some sugar and coffee and flour (which he had no use for) a bayonet, a tin cup, a spoon, and a canteen that he usually hung around his neck.

He brought out the gold coins, stacked them in even piles and started to count them. Each handful grabbed the orange, blue and yellow flames from the fireplace and reflected it into his eyes that were more alive now than they had been since he started his trip. His ciphering was never that good in school, but he knew there were more than fifty coins. Like the moon, his excitement was waning and fatigue was creeping in, so he decided to sleep until the sun came up where he could do more exploring and see if he could figure out where he was. He was almost sure that he was in Michigan and that was a good feeling. As he got up from the table his boot shuffled in the dirt floor and his heel caught on something. He looked down and saw that there was a wood plank under the dirt. He cleared some more dirt away with his boot and saw what appeared to be a small door under the dirt. He grabbed his bayonet and pried up the wood panel, reached down and pulled on the wood and he was right – it was a small door. He peered down. It was pitch black. An acrid smell of damp dirt invaded his nostrils. He walked over to the fireplace and found one of the pieces of wood he had gathered earlier and lit the end of it. He quickly went back to the hole, shielding the flame with one hand. He held the end of the handmade torch down and moved it around. He could see that there was a crude ladder down into a five-foot-high crawl space. *Probably a root cellar,* he thought. This gave him an idea. He was getting more paranoid as he got closer to Yankee territory and he was still wearing his Confederate-Grey uniform and had a pile of gold. What if he ran into the worst of the Yankees? All would be lost. His thought was to get down into the room, bury most of the coins, keep some to get him started and once he felt safe, he would return and collect the rest of the booty. *Good Plan*, he thought.

It was getting lighter outside and the cloudless sky was filtering in more light through the glassless window. He opened the door for even more light. He grabbed his haversack with all the contents he had just inventoried and placed it next to the opening of the root cellar. He gingerly stepped on the first rung of the ladder, tested its strength and then proceeded to get his feet to the bottom. He stooped and looked around and found that indeed it was a root cellar. There were stone crocks on the floor containing a variety of rotting carrots, potatoes and beets. He emptied out one of the crocks, stuck his head through the opening in the floor and scooped out handfuls of the gold coins from his haversack and neatly packed the crock full, leaving enough coins in his haversack for his new start in life. He grabbed his bayonet, loosened the dirt and with his hands he scooped out a hole big enough and deep enough to accommodate the crock so that the top of the crock would be well below the surface of the dirt floor. He put the cover back on the crock full of his cache and lowered it into the hole. He carefully filled in the hole with dirt, stomped on it and evened it over so as not to give any hint that something had been buried there. He thought that even if someone discovered the root cellar, they wouldn't find his concealed crock of treasure. He re-covered the opening with the wood door, smoothed it over with dirt, gazed at his work and relaxed on the homemade chair for some well-earned rest. In his haste, he failed to notice one of the coins that he accidently dropped and was now covered with dirt!

After relaxing in the chair for a few minutes and thinking of his treasure, he was invigorated by his action to secure his treasure and decided to venture out – explore – and rest later. The sun was rising and was filtering through the trees. As he looked around to get a feeling for his surroundings, he noticed that next to the woods that skirted the cabin, there were rows of uniform trees next to a copse of birch trees behind the cabin. There were at least ten rows of apple trees spreading out toward the horizon. The cabin made sense now that he saw that an abandoned apple orchard was evidently the reason for the cabin. He started to walk and think. He thought of why this place was abandoned? Was it because of the war? Was the owner drafted into the Union Army? *Probably both*, he thought. As he walked down one of the aisles between two rows of trees, he noticed that some of the apples started to fall and covered the ground knocking down some of the overgrown brush and weeds. The odor from the ripe apples was overwhelming and pleasant. It reminded him of the apple pies his sister often baked when he was living with her. He kicked the apples as he walked – looking for some of the better ones – not wormy or bruised. He picked one up, looked it over and wiped it on his jacket sleeve. As he bit into the juicy Jonathan apple, the juice ran down his chin. He ignored it and quickly bit his way around the entire apple. He tossed the core and continued his search for the best of the forsaken crop. When he had filled his haversack to the brim and eaten his fill, he wandered back to the cabin.

After a long nap and his stomach still full of delicious apples, he decided he would have to leave this haven and continue the trek toward a reunion with his family. He gathered all of his belongings on the makeshift table, checked under the table to make sure the dirt was covering the entrance to the root cellar sufficiently, looked at the fireplace that was still smoldering and started to pack up all of his belongings. As he lifted the haversack by its strap, he could feel the weight with the apples that added to the weight of the gold coins. He slung it over his shoulder so that it would rest on his side under his arm. The bed roll at the top gave him some cushion for the journey he was about to resume. He had previously filled his canteen with crystal clear lake water and he put the canteen strap over his neck and rested it under his arm opposite his haversack. *All set! Here we go*, he thought.

He figured on heading back to the sandbar to make his way back to the lake shoreline and head north again. He had crossed the sandbar getting to the island so there was no worry heading back the same way. He removed his brogans and stuffed his socks into his boots noticing that the heels on the socks were almost worn through. He tied the shoelaces together and slung the brogans over his shoulder. The feel of the sand on his weary feet was once again refreshing. As he reached the middle of the sandbar, he could feel the sand shifting more than the natural movement he felt with his footsteps. He looked down and to his right where he felt the most movement and was surprised to see an abyss of brownish green water. As he tried to steady his balance and hurry to the shore ahead of him, he felt the sand shifting even more. And it carried him into the lake!

The water was ice cold and soaked his heavy-woolen army uniform within seconds. He struggled to stay afloat and grab for the sandbar, but the more he struggled the faster he sank. He tried to remove the boots, canteen and haversack – but they were entwined around his neck and – the more he pulled and pushed on the straps – the more entangled they became. He freed one of his arms from the haversack but the weight of all the gear was too much to overcome. As it dragged him down and he lost the last of his breath – darkness entered his consciousness and quickly turned to nothingness and remained there forever!

1

The lake is called Lake Bilasaana – *lake shaped like an apple*. The Navajo Native Americans looked at the lake from a hill overlooking the lake and saw that the shape of the lake resembled an apple. It covered nearly 800 acres with a small feeder stream at the southern end that represented the stem of the apple. Over 100 feet deep in spots with a twenty-five-acre island. The spring fed lake teems with all varieties of bass, northern pike, catfish, perch and bluegill.

It was Shane's solace in good times and in troubling times.

He was somewhat of an enigma for a fourteen-year entering into those difficult years of puberty. His body was starting to develop more muscle over the baby-fat. He was sprouting up showing signs he inherited from his father's 6'2" height and was already taller than his mother. He had his father's and mother's good looks and blond hair. He was nerdy on one side of his personality that enjoyed reading and an insatiable appetite for exploring the mysteries of nature. This curiosity could rise to nearly obsessive if there was a question in his mind, he couldn't find the answer to – like – are UFOs real? He would not rest until he had an answer. The other side of his persona was a popular, athletic, handsome teenager with a smile that unarmed any one he talked with – especially the girls in his social circle, but not a steady girlfriend - yet! He excelled in most any sport he took an interest in, like basketball, baseball, football and pickup hockey games on Lake Bilasaana – but fishing was his favorite. Tips from his father Alan, got him started in his fishing passion. His inquisitive nature drove him into mastering the bait-cast rod and reel, the Palmer knot and the Texas rig to keep his line from snagging on weeds. It took all of his patience to master the cast and overcome the bird nests in the reel when he failed to put his thumb on the reel in time.

Being alone on a quiet sunrise, watching a warm breeze sweep across the lake and brush his face and feel the jerk on his line were the times on the lake that he enjoyed the most. He never thought about it consciously. It was just there. Maybe when he got older, he would think back and treasure these days as they morphed into memories?

The lake was quiet and serene, and the depth gave it a calming grayish-green sheen on sunny days. The

bucolic vistas were both calming and exciting, especially in the fall when the trees would light up with
nature's pallet of colors . . . from the intense reds of
the sugar and Japanese maples to the gold-coin yel-
lows of oaks and American elms and clump birch. The
traffic on the lake was limited to electric trolling mo-
tors, paddle boats, rowboats and kayaks – so it was a
quiet lake except for the laughing and splashing that
amplified across the lake from the swimming beaches
in the summer months. Springtime territorial swan
aggression to keep the Canada geese off the lake was
a dance to behold. The geese were no match for the
mate-for-life swan couples, especially when cygnets
hatched in early spring. The cob would fiercely and
aggressively chase off any geese that got near to the
pen and cygnets.

The homes on the lake varied from estate size
homes to moderate size ranches, with each lot having at least an acre to spread out on. Shane and his
mother and father enjoyed a two-acre lot with a three
thousand square foot split-level home. Looking out of
the twin picture-windows on either side of the door
wall in the family room, provided a vista that was void
of any structures – as if they were alone on their own
private lake.

During the summer Shane enjoyed the months
away from school. He enjoyed school and all the

challenges of learning something new and the companionship of his friends, but summer was his time. Learning and sports and companionship would be there soon enough.

Fall was on the horizon when his father Alan, approached Shane with an offer.

"Shane . . . my son, how about we take on a project for the winter?"

"Oh-oh! I don't like the sound of this." Shane replied to his father. They were in the garage at the time and Shane was afraid that his dad was going to assign him to clean out the garage or some other unwelcome ugly task.

"No. It's not like that. I think you might enjoy it. And . . . I will be helping you with it. What do you say?" Alan asked as he saw the apprehension building in Shane's face.

"You have to tell me what it is first."

"Okay. I was just testing you to see if you trusted me without knowing what the project was."

Alan Krieger was in his late forties. He was tall and fit. His job of Quality Control Director for an automotive up-fitting company kept him on the road quite a bit but he worked out at the gym and at home whenever he could. On some of the lonesome times on the road he would even find a workout place in the motel spa or close by.

"So, here's the proposal for the project. I found an old rowboat that has been sitting idle across the lake. It's Mr. Sampson's. He's getting up in age and his rowboat has been sitting overturned on the shore for a couple of years. I ran into him last week and asked him if he would be willing to sell it. I know you have been bugging me to buy a boat, but I thought we could work on it together and it could be fun. What do you think?"

"Hmmm. Sounds interesting but what do we know about restoring a boat. How bad is it?"

"Pretty bad. We'll . . . I should say you will have to do some research online to see the best way to do it. Agreed?"

"Agreed. Let's go see it or pick it up or whatever," Shane was starting to get excited about it. They got in Alan's Ford Explorer SUV and drove around the lake on the residential road that circled the lake and had access to all the cul-de-sacs in the Lake Bilasaana sub-division.

Mr. Sampson was blowing off the leaves that were beginning to cover the driveway. They greeted each other and Alan asked about the boat.

"It's yours for free if you want it. It's in pretty nasty shape and I probably won't be using it. I can give you some tips Shane, on how to restore it if that's what you're going to do," Mr. Sampson offered.

They loaded the boat on the roof of Alan's SUV, tied it down and slowly drove back home. Although Shane's original fear of cleaning out the garage was not the original project, it evolved into a necessity in order to get the boat into the three-car garage. They had a space heater available so working in the cold months wouldn't be too much of a hardship.

The 12-foot-long rowboat was in worse shape than Shane thought it was. In the garage sitting upside down on wooden saw-horses revealed a hull that would need a lot of fairing (a word that Shane learned from his research on-line. It meant sanding and restoring the natural shape of the boat from stem to stern). Shane was getting anxious and excited and as he did with most of interests, he jumped in with both feet. He went online and scoured all of the sites that gave tips and processes for restoring wooden boats. He spent time with Mr. Sampson and took notes on what he thought the best process would be. Dad was taxed with buying all the required supplies and tools, sandpaper, an electric sander, putty knives and scrapers, caulking, paint and mineral spirits, deck varnish, tack clothes and respirator masks.

Shane jumped right in as soon as he had the process down pat and had all the supplies. It turned out to be a one-man job instead of the joint project that Alan had originally proposed. Dad was just there on the weekends to observe the process and give Shane moral support. Shane didn't mind. He was taking personal pride in "his" boat. He spent enough time at school with his friends so when he got home, he did whatever homework he had and hurriedly raced into the garage, turned on the space heater and continued his work of passion.

The process went like this;

- The first thing he did was to clean the boat as best he could with a broom and rags to get all the surface dirt off
- He applied a wood stripper and carefully scraped all of the old paint and mold off of all the surfaces. He would concentrate on the exterior of the boat first and take care of the interior last. The interior was in much better shape.
- Once he was done with the paint stripping, he cleaned the surface again.
- Next was sanding and caulking any open joints
- Once the sanding and caulking and fairing was complete, he applied three coats of wood stain to bring out the natural colorful streaks in the wood.
- The last step was to apply wood varnish
- And on the completion, he rested and took pride in his accomplishment.

Cheryl and Alan had been married for sixteen years. It was as close to ideal as you could get. With Alan's job as a director, and her job as real estate agent, they afforded an idyllic and comfortable life on Lake Bilasaana. Aside from the comfortable life and rewarding marriage, Shane was the diamond in their marriage. He gave them pride in most of everything he did.

Spring was breaking and the forsythia bushes gushed their brilliant yellow on the border of their lot. Cheryl came home in early afternoon and saw Shane in the garage working on the interior of his boat.

"Wow! I never would believe it's the same P-O-S that you and your father dragged home. It's beautiful," she said as she walked next to the boat and rubbed her hand along the hull. She walked next to Shane and put her hand on his shoulder. "Almost finished?"

"What's with the P-O-S talk? Getting up with the social media acronyms? Pretty cool Mom. And yes, I'm close. I just need to clean up the transom-seat and get some new oarlocks and tholes for the oars,' Shane said as he gave his mother a devilish grin.

"I have no idea what you just said. Showoff."

"I can clue you in on all the new words I learned since I took on this project. You can use them in your crossword puzzles."

"Now that you mention it Shane, I do know what a thole is from my puzzles. It's the pin on an oar that fits into the oarlock. Right?"

"You got it Mom."

They hugged and Cheryl went into the house to start dinner and wait for Alan to get home. She wanted to eat out on the deck today now that the weather was warming up. Shane kept smiling from his warming conversation with his mother.

Cheryl made salad and mixed up some hamburger with their favorite spices and formed enough patties to feed them all. Alan was the chef when it came to the barbecue. Cheryl did all the indoor cooking. They all did their usual tasks in getting the meal ready and sat down at the patio table and enjoyed their first outdoor meal for the year.

"So, Shane, how far along are you on the boat? When will you be done?" Alan asked as they all finished eating.

"Almost done. You need to take me to the marine store on the weekend to get some new brass oarlocks and tholes. Ask Mom if you don't know what they are." Shane said and nodded his head at his mother.

"I know what they are smarty-pants. Yeah, we can go to the boat place on the weekend. And then we need to plan for the christening of your boat."

The boat was faired and finished with all shiny new brass hardware. They planned the christening for the following Friday evening. Shane's closest friends and some of their neighbors would be invited and a barbecue would follow the ceremony. True to Shane's philosophy to do everything complete and correct he looked up the proper steps for the christening event.

He would have a branch of the forsythia bush in the bow for good luck. He would have one of Mom's red wines in a burlap sack. He knew to avoid Friday (The day that Christ died) and Thursday (Thor's day, the god of thunder and lightning) for boat christenings!

Cheryl was given the honors!

"I christen thee *Cheryl Ann*. May you bring safety and fortune to all who board you."

She broke the bottle of red wine on the bow that Shane had protected with a thick piece of canvas. She walked along the dock that the boat was moored at and stared at the name that Shane had given her – *Cheryl Ann*. A tear trickled down her face. She wiped it away and hugged the two most important people in her life.

2

It would be the maiden voyage for the *Cheryl Ann*. Shane enjoyed the christening of his boat and enjoyed all the kudos from his friends, neighbors and relatives that joined the celebration. The following morning, he rose early – beating the sun by half an hour. He quietly got dressed and had a light breakfast of maple and brown sugar oatmeal, a piece of toast, and a glass of orange juice. He went into the garage and collected his tackle box, a spinning rod and his favorite Lews Mach II Bait caster, already rigged with a bright orange rubber worm fixed onto an offset hook for a perfect Texas rig. The spinning rod was taken for backup and would wait for the ubiquitous bird nest on his bait caster to show up.

By the time he got all his gear into to his new boat, the sun was peeking through the trees on the far side of the lake. The ducks, geese and swans had not yet started to stir. It was just Shane – his own private boat – his own private lake.

His eventual destination would be Orchard Island.

In the past he would have to depend on one of his friends on the lake to take him over to the island. Most of them didn't have Shane's passion to explore so they would drop him off on the island and pick him up in a few hours. The alternative was to try to get one of the few paddleboats that the Lake Association had for communal use. This was usually a frustrating wait for someone to return with a paddleboat so he could make his way over to the island.

Now his newfound freedom to explore and independence to come and go as he pleased had him excited. He loaded the boat with his gear, a life jacket and two bottles of water and set sail.

The lake was still, not a breeze to be felt. The morning fog was melting into the mirror surface of the lake and was reflecting the orange sun and peach colored sky as the boat slid across the lake. Shane decided to fish for a while, see what happens and then make his way over to the island. The oars in the oarlocks squeaked a little at first, but then quieted as they found and polished their new surroundings. He was pleased with his work and smiled to himself in this personal accomplishment. A little WD-40 might be needed later for the oars. His concern now was if he had done a good enough job on the fairing and caulking. He kept his eyes on the decking toward the transom and occasionally turned his head toward the bow to look for any leaks. So far so good! He knew from all his research that the wood would swell a bit, once it sat in the water, and take care of any small leaks that might be in the making.

After only a few casts and no bird nests he got a nice tug on the line. He set the hook and reeled in a nice two to three-pound smallmouth bass. He carefully removed the hook from the bass's lip and eased it back into the lake and tried for more. His success was overwhelming, and he was starting to get bored with the ease of catching good-sized fish on this perfect morning. He lost his concentration and 'voila' a bird nest on his reel. That did it. He didn't want to fool with what usually was a frustrating attempt to fix the tangle of monofilament, so he leaned the rod and reel against the seat – stared at the mess to fix later – and headed toward the island.

He had tied a water ski rope to an eyelet screw he screwed into the gunwale at the bow of the boat. He didn't feel he needed an anchor yet, so the rope could be used for mooring the boat. He rowed his way around the island, keeping an eye out for a tree close enough and a shoreline clear enough so he could tie-up and get onto the island. He spotted a copse of birch trees growing right next to the shore and a small sandy clearing. He was wearing Crocs water shoes so stepping into the water was not a problem. He tied the rope to one of the birches, checked to see everything was secure, grabbed his water bottle and proceeded to start a tour around the island.

In his past excursions he was always hurried. So . . . this time he would take his time and walk around the perimeter of the island and see what he could find. There wasn't a steady path around the edge of the island, so he had to zig-zag to make his way around. He had heard that there was an old abandoned cabin somewhere on the island and he was hoping he could find it. He didn't have any fear of getting lost. All he had to do was follow the shoreline to find his boat.

As the sun got higher in the sky and he fought some of the brush and bushes around the shoreline he started to get a little tired. Time to take a rest and get his bearings. There was a good-sized log perfectly close to the shore. It was close to a sand bar that reached from the island to the lake shoreline. He knew about the sandbar from past trips. It was common knowledge amongst the serious fishermen on the lake that the deep spot next to the sandbar was notorious for swallowing up plugs and all sorts of fishing rigs and gear. The unanimous theory was that there was a fallen tree or roots that spread out from the island that was devouring the gear. There was also an old legend that someone had drowned there a long time ago! He sat down and put his feet in the water to cool them off. He took a swig of water. The water was warm by now and not very refreshing. He put the cap back on and pushed the half-filled plastic bottle into the sandy shoreline next to his foot, hoping to cool the water a bit. He put his hands behind his head and leaned back and enjoyed the view and his little exploration of the island. *Enough for today. There will be many more days to explore*, he thought.

As he was getting ready to make his way back to his boat, he noticed something hanging on a willow branches that was drooping into the water. He waded over and with his thumb and forefinger he plucked it off the branch. He lifted it and twirled it around and grimaced. It was a woolen sock that had seen better days. He noticed that the heel was almost worn through. Rather than throw it back on the island or into the lake he would practice his eco-friendly spirit and take it back with him and throw it in the trash. It was not unusual for him to go after trash he spotted in the lake and make a reasonable effort to do his part in keeping the lake clean.

His mother Cheryl was sitting on the deck overlooking the lake as Shane returned from his fishing and excursion to Orchard Island. She was wearing her usual summer-at-home outfit: Bermuda shorts, a loose-fitting tee shirt and flip-flops, short blond streaky hair drying from her morning shower. She was sipping on a cup of coffee and enjoying the late morning warmup.

Shane noticed her and gave her a wave as he unloaded his gear and threw the old sock on shore.

"What'd you catch Shane?"

"Plenty of bass and this old sock," he answered as he held up the sock with two fingers.

Cheryl laughed and waved at him and patted the chair next to her, signaling him to come sit with her. Shane was entering that age where teen-agers started to shy away from kissing or hugging their parents. Shane never gave that a second thought. He was always close to his mother and father. Even closer to his mother when it came to personal issues and struggles. Dad was there for questions on sports or fixing something, but Mom was the one he could depend on for reasonable and helpful answers about girls, friends, school issues and even social media questions.

After a peck on the cheek, Shane sat down across from his mother and grabbed one of the bottles of water on the patio table. He unscrewed the top and drank half of the bottle with one gulp.

"Pretty thirsty I see. Where you been other than fishing?

"I took a small tour of the island. I always wanted

to do that without having to depend on Denny or someone else to take me over there."

"Find anything interesting?"

"Nothing but that old sock if you want to call that interesting? I'll be doing a lot more over the summer. I heard there's an old collapsed cabin somewhere over there. I'd like to see that and see what the history is. You're in real estate Mom; can you find out who owns the island or owned it and see if you can find out any history about it going back as far as you can? Do you have access to plats? Is that what you call them?"

"Yes, plats describe lots or pieces of property. I do get access to county, city plat records at times. I'll take a look when I go back to work and get some time. How's that?"

"Great. No hurry. I've got another month of school till I do some serious exploring. Speaking of work. I know Dad's at work. What are you doing home to-day? Saturdays are usually your busy days for showing houses. Playing hooky?"

"I'm not feeling well. I've been having some pains in my side. I've got an appointment with my female doctor on Monday. I hope it's not an appendix or a kidney stone. I just need to get it checked out."

"I'm sure it's nothing Mom. You look as healthy as a horse . . . whatever that means. I'm going in to shower and get the fish smell off me. Do you need anything?"

"No. I'm fine," Cheryl smiled and watched Shane go in through the door wall. As the screen door shut, she grabbed her side and grimaced. She knew it was something serious. She was hoping it was an appendix or a kidney stone that could easily be fixed. She would just have to put up with it until Monday and try not to worry Shane or Alan too much.

3

It was a typical Sunday for the Krieger family. They weren't overly religious but they did stick to a routine of Mass at Saint Mary, Our Lady of the Snows, in Milford, on Sunday, and usually brunch at one of the local restaurants. They took turns on choosing where they would eat. It was Shane's turn so he picked his usual, Americus Coney Island, where he could order his favorite of two Coney dogs, an order of fries and a coke. Little was discussed as far as Cheryl's health except that she had an appointment with her gynecologist tomorrow. Cheryl and Alan spent the rest of the day planting flowers, raking the lawn while Shane did a little fishing and rowed to, and around Orchard Island.

Cheryl went to her gynecologist that Monday and got a complete female exam. Dr. Hammoud talked to her about her side ache, how long she had it and how she was feeling other than the side ache. She said she would order blood work — a complete panel — and she would schedule an MRI and upper and lower GIs within the next week. There was some small talk about Shane and Alan as Dr. Hammoud tried to put Cheryl at ease knowing that the side ache Cheryl was describing could be an ovary. And that would probably mean only one thing!

Cheryl left the doctor's office even more worried than when she went in. Cheryl was not a worry wart. She usually took things in stride and was the one who would calm things down when Alan was having problems at work or Shane was worrying about school tests or sports' disappointments. When Dr. Hammoud ordered up MRI and GI tests within the next week she knew that these types of tests were usually ordered months in advance. There were always long waiting lists for limited hospital space and expensive MRI machines — this was serious!

The day was sunny and bright unlike her disposition. She decided to go to work and try to occupy her mind until she received a call about an appointment for the tests.

She worked at Real Estate One offices in Union Lake. It was a moderate size office with ten agents alternating at answering any prospective clients. She said the routine 'hellos' and 'how's its goings' to the men and women that were in their open cubicles and settled in to her cubicle. She made a few calls to set up some showings and got her listings up to date. Her mind was occupied, and her medical issues were pushed to the back of her brain – for now.

Around lunch time she told the receptionist at the lobby that she would be gone for the afternoon but would have her cell phone on for any calls she needed to take. She decided to get a quick bite at McDonalds that was in the same mini-mall as Real Estate One offices. As she finished up her fish sandwich and salad, she decided to head over to the county clerk's office to do some research on Orchard Island for Shane. See what she could dig up.

She was familiar with the location of the Oakland County Clerk's office from visits she made there in the past to search for various property information. It was located in the Oakland County office complex. She asked the clerk for a copy of the plat for Orchard Island and any information about the owners, previous owners and anything else she could find. The clerk helped her with getting a copy of the plat but told her that searching through the microfilm on file was on her. She showed her how to use the microfilm and microfiche on the microfilm machine; how to load film or microfiche, how to focus and zoom and print at ten cents a copy.

Once she got comfortable with the machine, she got enthused about researching and getting some history of Orchard Island for Shane, once again taking her mind off of her health questions.

After she finished making copies, she sat down at one of the large library-style table-desks and started reading through all of the copies and hi-lighting what she thought Shane would be interested in.

After she got home, she put on some casual, comfy clothes, grabbed a bottle of water from the fridge and went on the deck and waited for Shane to get home from school. She was looking at the documents she printed out and was hoping he would get home right after school so she wouldn't have to stare at the lake and let all kind of uncomfortable thoughts invade her brain. He was late – so the ugly thoughts came. She looked down at her evenly tanned legs that she had propped up on one of the wicker-patio chairs. *Could I have spent too much time in the sun? Is it something hereditary?* She tried to think of any of her female relatives that had anything she should be worried about. Her mother had breast cancer and had a radical mastectomy. She had two sisters, one older and one younger. She didn't know of any serious women problems with them. Her mind was racing, and she was getting scared. At the peak of her nervousness, she heard Shane open the door wall screen door. Distraction at last!

"Hi Mom. Playing hooky again? You're going to get fired." Shane laughed as he put his hand on her shoulder and bent down and kissed her lightly on the cheek. He loved the smell of Shalimar that she used most every day.

"Hey . . . I've been busy. Doctor, work at the office and most important I spent the afternoon at the County Clerk's office doing your research." She said pointing at the small stack of papers on the glass top patio table.

"How did the doctor go?"

"Don't know yet. She needs to take some tests later this week or next week. I'll let you know."

"Let me get changed and you can show me what you got." Shane said and turned and went back into the house. He quickly got out of his school clothes, put on shorts, a vintage Pink Floyd tee shirt and flip-flops. He was anxious to see what his mother had collected for him.

"Okay Mom. Let's see what you got for me."

Cheryl grabbed the pile of about twenty pages and handed them to Shane. "I printed out whatever I could find on the microfiche and microfilm and then I hi-lighted whatever I thought might interest you. You won't have to read all of it if you don't want to."

"What the heck is a microfiche? Is that something you can catch in Lake Bilasaana?" They both laughed.

"Yeah, I guess you and your friends wouldn't know what microfiche is. You guys go to Google whenever you want to find something. There was a technical world before your fancy phones and laptops. So . . . microfiche are pieces of flat film with reduced size images that you put into a microfilm machine and you can search for whatever, and print it out when you find it. If you're really curious I can take you down to the clerk's office or you can go to the library. Most libraries still use them although not so much with all the new technology."

As Cheryl was talking Shane was leafing through the pages and stopping to read when a hi-lighted area caught his eye.

"Thanks Mom. I really appreciate it. Looks like you got some interesting stuff here that'll help me with my exploration of the island."

The weather started to change. The sky that started as sunny and bright gradually changed to grey and ominous. Thunderheads were building in the west and a storm was surely on its way. Shane figured he may as well take advantage of the bad weather and read in detail what his mother gave him.

He went into his room to do some research. His room was not the typical 14-year-old boy's room. He was very meticulous with most everything in the room; desk with a neat pile of schoolwork and a neat pile of research on whatever sparked his interest at the time, clothes neatly hung or folded and put into specific drawers, books sorted by subject matter in his bookshelf etc., etc. He was using the pull-out trundle bed – once used for stay-overs when he was much younger – to store some of his sports equipment; bats and gloves, helmets and rollerblades, footballs and soccer balls.

He sat down at his desk and dropped his stack of schoolwork and books on the floor and started to read the island material. He had a note pad and hi-lighter at the ready. As he read, he made notes on what interested him and what he might need for his exploration of the island.

When he read through the microfiche copies twice and made notes, he read through the notes that lit up his imagination on what he might find on the island. He plopped on his bed and placed the notes on his pillow and began to read his notes:

Formed during last ice age, 10,000 to 12,000 years ago

Over 400 species of flora

Native Americans of different tribes inhabited
the island at various times

37 Acre Island – three-eighths of a mile in
length and a quarter of a mile in width

Highest point 960 feet in elevation above sea
level and 31 feet above lake level

Found on island; wampum, pewter, hammer-
stones, arrowheads, carvings of birds

Folklore about Chief Pontiac buried there at
one time — then moved

Originally called Menahsagorning – "apple
place" in Native American

William Dow built a cabin and raised apples in
orchard there in early 1800s

These were the broad notes that he made. What
really caught his eye were three things. One – that
there was a cabin there but it was flattened in 1978
when one of the worst blizzards to hit the Midwest
produced over two feet of snow and up to 80 mph
winds. Two – that the national Register of Historic
Places along with the Michigan Historic Preservation

Network Society are in the works of designating Orchard Island as a historic site by the end of the year and they cautioned – After *this – all traffic to the island will be monitored and any excavation or archaeological digs would have to be approved by the local government*. Three – The Temperate Orchard Conservancy located in Oregon would be investigating the apples found on Orchard Island as part of The Lost Apple Project – A project to locate and identify apple varieties that were believed to be extinct.

This told him he would have to finish any exploring he wanted to do by the end of summer!

Cheryl received a call from Dr. Hammoud later that week. She told her that she was unable to schedule her MRI and GI's until later in the month. The machines and labs were backed up.

"What does that mean Doctor?"

"Not to worry. Your blood work shows everything normal. However, I would like for you to come in for one more blood test. It's a CA125."

"What's that for?"

"It's just to be on the safe side until we can get the other test scheduled. It's a cancer antigen test for ovarian cancer. I don't want you to worry. How is your pain since I saw you?"

"Not bad. In fact, it seems to have gone away for the most part."

"That's good and a good sign. So just come in for the blood test and I'll let you know as soon as I get the word on when the other tests are available. You don't have to see me. Just go to the lab here and the orders will be there for the CA125 test. Okay?"

"Okay. But I'm worried now that you asked for this blood test."

"I don't want to worry you Cheryl, but I just want to make sure we're doing everything we need to, to keep you safe."

"Okay. Thank you, doctor," Cheryl said and quietly ended the call. She would go for the blood test and try not to worry about it, but that would be almost impossible. She would just have to occupy her mind with work and spending as much time as she could with Alan and Shane.

4

School was out for the summer and Shane was getting antsy to get in some fishing. It was a Saturday morning, and he was loading up his boat with his usual gear. Looked like a three-bottle water day. The sun was halfway up and heating the lake. The fish would be staying deeper so he didn't get up his hopes up of having his usual success. He also planned on doing some exploring, if fishing got too boring. As he finished putting in his tackle box, two poles, a small bag with water and a package of peanut butter cheese crackers, he was startled by an approaching boat. He didn't hear it coming. It was his best friend, Denny Rashid.

Denny was in his flat-bottomed ten-foot aluminum fishing boat with an electric trolling motor. He guided the boat up to the sandy shore until it wouldn't go any further.

"Gonna do some fishing Sak?" Sak was the nickname that Shane had acquired from his friends. They took his full names initials, Shane Alan Krieger, to form his nickname. At times of key hits in a baseball game, they would shout Sak, Sak! Shane was okay with the nickname as long as they didn't overdo it. Dad liked it. Mom, not so much.

"Yeah, I want to get out before it gets too hot. What about you? What are you up to?"

"Just trolling around the lake. No luck."

"Why don't we head over to "The Hole" next to the sandbar? I haven't been in your fancy new boat yet, so you can row us over there."

"Okay. Just grab your rods. There's not enough room for your big-ass tackle box. You can use my lures. But I'm not sure about going over to "The Hole". You know that place has a knack for snagging everything you drop down there – it's like there's a magnet down there."

"Not to worry. If I lose any of your precious lures, I'll give you one of mine. And I hear from my dad that some lunkers have been hauled in from there lately."

"Okay Denny. Hop in and let's go."

Denny was not quite the physique of Shane. More on the portly side with freckles and brown stick-out hair – no matter how he tried to comb it or hair spray it down.

As Shane rowed, Denny sat on the transom-seat with his hands behind his head, enjoying the free ride, the sun, and the little breeze blowing across the lake. Shane rowed around the island to the far side so they could approach "The Hole" next to the sandbar. He didn't have any anchor yet, so they tied the bow of the boat to some shoreline birches and let the boat drift until it was parallel to "The Hole".

Denny helped himself to one of Shane's bright green iridescent deep-dive Rapala plugs. He put some lead shot on the line to take it down deep and hoped for the best. Shane stuck to his proven Texas rig with a bobber and his bait cast rod and reel.

It only took Shane a few casts until he pulled in a smallmouth bass worthy of mounting. Denny waited patiently and watched Shane pull in two or three more with a wry look on his face.

"You gonna fish or just sit there with that plug halfway down to hell?"

"Yeah, I guess I'll try a little closer to the surface." Denny started to reel in his line with a slow and steady reel. After a half a dozen turns, he felt a tug. He tried to set the hook but quickly realized it was a snag and not a bite.

"Damn. I knew it. It's caught on something Sak. I'll try to get it in but I may lose it."

"You'll owe me."

"I know," Denny replied as he tugged and tugged and watched his rod bend to the limit. And then the line snapped, and he fell backward – almost out of the boat.

"Oh well. Like you said, I owe you one. You can choose one from my box when we get back or I'll buy you a new Rapala."

As Shane was rowing back to his house and Denny's boat, Denny said. "I just had an idea. You're a good swimmer Shane . . . swim team and all that. How about if we come back one day and you go down there with some snorkel gear and see what you can see. Maybe even get your plug back. Don't know what you'll find down there. Wha'd ya say Sak?"

"You're crazy Denny. I'll eat the plug if you don't want to pay me for it."

"Okay chicken. I was just thinking. It would be like diving into the water around that island hole at Sawgrass and scooping up golf balls, except you could be scooping up fishing gear. Just saying."

The rest of the trip was in silence and the day was heating up.

Back at shore Denny took his rods, thanked Shane, and offered him a lure, which he declined, got in his boat and silently motored back to his house.

The seed that Denny planted was starting to root in Shane's inquisitive mind. What if I dove down there a little way and see what kind of gear was down there and what was snagging all that gear? He would think about it for a little while before he developed a plan. He would talk to Denny.

Denny's idea of diving for his gear was getting stronger. It was gnawing at Shane's curiosity gene. He went into the garage to see if he still had his mask and snorkel that he used on the family's last trip to Hawaii. All three of them took some lessons on how to use the snorkel to breath with floating and how to dive without taking in a mouthful of water. He readily found the mask and snorkel and a pair of rubberized diving gloves, also a dive knife in a black ABS sheath that his father had bought for the macho in him. Shane grabbed the mask and snorkel and the sheath with the knife and gloves and wandered out onto the deck.

He was inspecting the knife, pulling it out of the sheath and snapping it back in and testing how the leg straps snapped to the leg with the adjustment slide. He was cleaning off the mask with a paper towel and some Windex when his mother came out onto the deck.

"What are you up to now Shane?" she asked as she sat across from him at the patio table.

"Just cleaning up some of this snorkel gear we used when we were in Hawaii."

"You going snorkeling on the lake?"

"Not really. I'm thinking about taking a dive over by "The Hole" to retrieve some fishing tackle Denny lost for me."

"That could be dangerous. You don't know what's down there. Don't go by yourself," she cautioned Shane.

"Don't worry. I'll have Denny with me. I'm just going to go down a little way – not real deep. What about your doctor stuff? Any new news?"

"I'm still waiting on some blood tests. Not to worry. I'll let you know as soon as I know something. You just go and have fun and be careful."

❦

He texted Denny and told him to come over that he had something to discuss. Denny was there in a half an hour.

"Hey Sak, what's up?"

"I've been thinking about your little idea about diving down to retrieve my fishing plug –and I dug my old snorkel mask and a dive knife my dad had and I think I'm going to give it a try. I need you to be on the boat with me. Just in case. I don't think anything can happen. I just want someone with me in case I need help. You in?"

"Yeah sure. I'm all for it. When do you want to go?"

"Right now. I'm going in to put on some swim trunks and you go home and do the same. I'll see you here in a little. Okay?"

"Okay."

Denny left and was back in half an hour and Shane was waiting by his boat.

Denny glanced down at the dive knife strapped on Shane's calf. "Got the knife and everything. Cool."

"Just in case I have to cut some line if I find some lures. Okay, let's go."

They got in the empty boat, except for some bottles of water, and Denny rowed over to the island while Shane played with the dive knife and spitting on the dive mask and rubbing it around and hoping it would prevent fogging when he went into the water.

When they got to the island, they tied up the boat to the same birch tree that they used on their last fishing trip where they lost the lure.

"Okay here goes" Shane said as he lowered the mask onto his face and moved it around to get it comfortable and sealed. While sitting on the middle seat he put his legs over the side of the boat, he grabbed the transom and pushed himself up and over and into the water. The water still held some of the winter's cold and forced him to let out a little gasp. He took a lung-full of air and waved at Denny and Denny gave him the thumbs-up sign and watched him sink down.

He peered over the side and watched as Shane turned his body head down and kicked – propelling him down into the abyss.

The water was still cool and clear, and Shane could see a good distance. He was aware he had only a short time he could hold his breath so he figured to get a lay of the land (or water if you will) – come up for air – and go back down to retrieve . . . whatever?

At ten feet or so, he saw what was snaring all the fishing equipment. A giant white pine tree had snapped at the base and toppled down into "The Hole". The extensive root system was what was keeping the sandbar from eroding into the lake. It was acting as a barrier and at the same time it was a seine. The now overturned tree was an unusual sight. Shane could see a variety of plugs, spinners, worm rigs and even bobbers scattered across the upside-down limbs of the tree. He spotted his favorite iridescent lure easily, as he was running out of breath. He headed for the shimmering, mirrored surface above.

Denny was waiting patiently as Shane's head popped out of the water next to the boat.

"Well, what did you see?"

Shane was gasping for breath and he held up his index finger as he sucked as much air as he could.

"It's a toppled over tree down there that's snagging everything. I think I saw my lure. I'm going back as soon as I get my breath. It looks like an upside-down Christmas display for a fishing sale at Bass Pro down there."

Shane stayed in the water with his elbows hanging inside the transom as Denny offered him a drink of water.

After he got his breath, he told Denny to give him the gloves. "I don't want to stick one of those treble hooks into my hand. I'll use these to be safe."

He spit on the mask again with a fresh coating of spittle, rubbed it around and put it back on his face. He signaled to Denny and Denny gave him the thumbs up once again and Shane slipped down into "The Hole".

He headed straight for his iridescent plug, reached down for the dive knife in the sheath on his calf and easily cut the monofilament. He spotted a few more interesting plugs and gathered them up in his gloved hand. Running out of breath again he started his ascent. As he approached the shadow of the boats hull, he looked down and saw what he thought was a back pack. No time to go back – he needed air.

As he got to the rail of the boat, he reached up his hand with the fishing plugs and Denny gingerly plucked then off the glove. "You done? Looks like a nice haul. Is there anything else down there?"

"I saw something else hanging on the tree. Looked like a backpack or something. I think I'll go down one more time after I catch my breath."

"You want to get in the boat and take a rest?"

"No, I'm good. Just need a few."

After a few minutes with his arms getting tired hanging over the transom, he once again slipped on the mask and took his third dive. He headed directly for the pack that he saw, ignoring any of the lures that remained on the tree. The object was near the top of the tree which was now toward the bottom of the lake. It was further down than the fishing lures and his breath was running out faster than the other dives. He grabbed the strap that was hooked on one of the branches and pulled as hard as he could. The strap selfishly hung on to the branch. Air getting short! He gave it another yank. This time the branch snapped, and the sack was free. He headed for much needed air, dragging the sack to his side, and kicking furiously to get to the surface.

He quickly threw the sack to Denny and grabbed onto the transom of the boat as he gasped for air.

"What the heck is this? It smells like shit," Denny said as he gingerly held the strap and carefully lowered it onto the deck of the boat.

Shane was getting his breath back. "I don't know what it is. Give me a hand to get back in the boat and we'll have a look." Denny grabbed Shane's arm and reached back and grabbed the waist of his bathing suit and helped him shimmy back on to the boat.

"Let me see that." Shane reached out his hand and Denny grabbed the strap with two fingers and handed it to Shane.

Shane undid the buckle on the pack and lifted the cover that had faded initials on the greenish brown canvas. A strong smell of rotting food wafted out. They both covered their noses. Shane peeked inside and saw what looked like rotten apples fused together in one clump. There were a couple of rotting crappies contributing to the stench. He leaned the pack on the side rail and gently shook the pack and watched the rotten apples and dead fish fall into the lake and sink toward the bottom. He took another peek and saw a straight piece of metal. He reached in and pulled it out. They both looked at it as Denny scratched his head. "What is that? Looks like some sort of bayonet."

"I think your right. It's an old bayonet."

He handed the bayonet to Denny and looked in the sack again. There was a small pouch he pulled out. It had drawstrings so he pulled on the opening to another smelly glob of rotting hardtack and jerky. He quickly dumped it into the lake and sloshed out the bag and put it down on the bottom of the boat. He looked down in the bag again and didn't see much, just some pieces of the rotting apples stuck to the bottom of the sack, so he grabbed the outside of the bottom of the bag and held it over the edge of the boat and shook it. They both gasped and couldn't act quick enough as they saw a few dingy gold flashes tinkle as they fell into the lake and quickly sank!

"OMG Shane! That looked like some coins! Did you see them?"

"I just caught a glimpse. Could have been coins. Too late now. And don't get any bright ideas about me going down there to get them. That hole is too deep. You would need scuba gear to go that deep. We'll never know. Let's head back. I want to dry all this stuff out and see if we can find out what it is, where it came from or whatever."

"I'll leave that up to you Shane. You're the detective. Just let me know if you find anything. What are you going to do with the fishing stuff you found? Any reward for the helper in this little excursion?"

"Yeah, sure. Take what you want. Just leave me my plug that we went down to get. You can have the rest."

"Thanks, Sak."

They headed back and docked the boat. Shane hung the sack and the little bag on one of the dock poles to dry out. He took the bayonet with him to show his mother and father and tell them about their little dive adventure.

Shane was excited. Not because he got his lure back but because he found what might be an antique bayonet. Cheryl was on the deck ready to welcome him and see what adventure he and Denny had at "The Hole", as the kids called it.

"Well . . . how did it go? Did you get your fish stuff back?"

"Yeah. Sure did. And . . . we found this old . . . mmmm bayonet I think." He handed the bayonet to his mother. She grabbed it and turned it slowly in her hands as she looked at it.

"Sure looks like a bayonet. Maybe from the Civil War. Could be worth a few bucks. Dad should be home in a few minutes. Show him and see what he thinks. We're cooking out again today. Such a nice day. I've got brats and homemade potato salad. You hungry?

"Sure am. I could eat a horse. Healthy as a horse – eat a horse – beat a dead horse – I wonder why the poor horses get all the bad idioms. Is that what those sayings are Mom? You do all those crosswords. You should know."

"Yes, those are idioms, but I don't know why the poor horses get all the bad stuff."

As they were discussing dead horses and such Alan came onto the deck. "What's with the dead horses you're talking about?"

"You had to be there Dad. We were just horsing around." Another giggle and Shane handed the bayonet to his father. I found this with Denny as we were trying to get one of my fishing lures out of "The Hole". What do you think it is? Don't say anything Mom. Let Dad tell us."

"It sure looks like an antique bayonet. Circa Civil War maybe?'

"That's what we think. Hold on. I found it in an old canvas sack. Let me go get it."

Shane ran down to the dock and plucked the sack off of the dock pole. He could feel that it was starting to dry. He brought it up to the deck and dropped it on the table.

"Get that dirty thing off the table Shane. We're going to eat there shortly. Let me see that thing." Cheryl grabbed the sack and carefully examined it like she did with the bayonet. "Do you know what this is Shane?" She pointed at the fading "CSA" initials. Shane shook his head. "It stands for The Confederate States of America, the bayonet and this haversack – that's what it's called – they fit together. Wow! Great find. Could be worth something on Antiques Roadshow?"

"Let me see that Cheryl." Alan asked.

He grabbed the haversack and opened the flap, pinched his nose shut and looked inside. "Did you know there is something else in here Shane?"

"What? More dead fish? I thought I cleaned it out. Sorry."

"Not dead fish. Something shiny. Take a look."

Shane took the haversack from his father and looked inside and – yes – there was something shiny and gold at the bottom peeking out from one of the sewn-over seams. He reached down and flicked it out from under the seam and held it between his thumb and forefinger and looked at both sides. He wet his other thumb and was about to wipe off some of the grime when his mother grabbed his hand.

"No.! Don't. Leave whatever patina is on the coin there. Sometimes antiques or old coins are worth more if they are left in the condition found. Let me see Shane."

Cheryl held the coin the same as Shane, on its edges with her thumb and forefinger. "This coin says United States of America – 1861-D, so it's probably not a CSA coin. The D is for the mint where it was minted. D for Denver, I guess? But I'm not sure that Denver was minting coins in 1861. Hang on." Cheryl went into the house taking the coin with her. She returned in a short while holding an Altoid tin with a black velvet jewelry pocket. She snapped it open and handed it to Shane along with the coin. "Keep it in here so you don't lose it. You've got a lot of research to do Shane. Then, maybe take it to a reputable dealer and see what they think."

"Okay, enough history lessons. I'm as hungry as a horse," Alan said.

Cheryl and Shane let out a synchronized guffaw.

5

Shane didn't waste any time. The next morning, he got up as the sun was peeking through the venetian blinds in his room. Still in his pajama bottoms and a Foo Fighters tee shirt, he opened his laptop and went right to Google. 1861-D was his first search. He scrolled and double clicked and hi-lighted and copied everything he could find on the coin his father found in the bottom of the haversack. The information was plentiful, and some was conflicting. He would have to sort out truth from fiction from Wikipedia un-vetted inaccuracies.

What he did learn, when he saw the same facts on more than one source was fascinating. The 1861-D coins were minted in the Dahlonega Mint in Georgia. The Mint was taken over by The Confederate Army in 1861. At least 1000 coins minted – could be up to 3,250? Dahlonega Mint produced coins for the Confederate States for only three months. At end of the war in 1865, the Confederate Army moved all the gold from the mint to prevent the Union Army from stealing it. The gold travelled by train and wagons to other cities in the South. Many rumors were running rampant, even to this day, as to what amount of gold was actually accounted for, what was stolen, what was used to pay soldiers, what was lost, etc., etc.? Shane's head was swimming with all kind of fantasies. Could this coin really be worth a lot of money if he decided to sell it? He wanted to do more research and felt that this would be a good time to go to the library and learn how to use the microfiche his mother told him about.

The curiosity that he had for exploring the island that had waned a bit, was re-kindled after he started to read about the history of the coin. He started to fantasize all sorts of scenario. From a cache of coins at the bottom of the lake to a buried chest somewhere on the island. Back to reality and see if Mom would help him at the library.

Alan had already left for work when Shane went into the kitchen. Cheryl was still in her pajamas, consisting one of Alan's Alice Cooper tee shirts and a pair of loose-fitting gym shorts. Her short Dorothy Hamill style hairdo didn't need much grooming after eight hours. Her hair always looked presentable!

"Good morning Mom. Sleep good?"

"Yes, thank you son. And you?"

"Been thinking a lot about that coin. You know . . . pirates' treasure and all that stuff. Anyway, I did some digging on Google this morning and found a lot of interesting things about that coin. If it's authentic it could be worth some money. And the D stands for the Dah . . . Dah . . . Dahlinga or something like that . . . I think . . . not sure how to pronounce it. It was a mint in Georgia that the Rebels captured."

"Very interesting. You need to dig as far as you can on this coin. And then take it to a reputable dealer and see what it's worth."

"That's exactly my plan. And I need your help. I want to go to the library and root through those fish files you talked about."

Cheryl laughed. "You mean microfiche. I'd be happy to. Let's have some breakfast. I'll shower and check in at work and then we can go."

Cheryl convinced Shane that a trip downtown to the Main Detroit Library would be the best and would probably have the best research data bases.

Shane was amazed at the size of the library. He was used to the economy sized libraries at school and in Commerce Township. They checked in at the main desk. Cheryl showed her driver's license since they didn't have library cards. With some help from one of the librarians they found their way to the micro-fiche and microfilm section. They found films going back to the early 1900's but that was it. They searched for Civil War – for gold coins – Dahlonega Georgia

– Dahlonega Mint – Confederate lost gold – but to no avail. They finally gave up. They went back to the main desk and asked for any book or books on gold coins from 1861.

"If you couldn't find anything in the micro files let me see what I can find," the be-speckled college age librarian offered.

"That would be great," Cheryl replied.

The librarian went to his computer, typed in a subject and came up with a list of books on Confederate gold. He printed it out with all the pertinent information including The Dewey Decimal identification number.

Shane took the list from the librarian, thanked him and said he would see if he could purchase one or two of these on Amazon. Cheryl took the list and said. "These two look interesting "Lost Confederate Gold by Robert C. Jones and Confederate Gold by Bill Westhead. You can order them on Amazon and put them on my Prime account Shane. If they have them, you can get them in one day."

"Thanks Mom."

They drove back home talking about the coin and what an interesting search this turned out to be starting with a snagged fishing plug.

The red-light on the answering-machine was flashing when they entered into the kitchen through the garage side door. Cheryl punched the flashing red-light button.

"This is Doctor Hammoud's office. This message is for Cheryl Krieger. Please call back on this number."

"Cheryl's pulse increased exponentially as she listened to the message. She immediately called back and asked to speak with Dr. Hammond's nurse.

"Hi Cheryl. This is Dr. Hammoud. I have the MRI scheduled for Friday. Because they may give you a sedative you will have to bring a driver. Is Alan available to come with you?"

"Yes Doctor. I'm sure he can drive me. Is there anything else going on with the blood test we took?"

"We can discuss everything on Friday. Okay? I'll see you then. I'll turn you over to the PA now and she'll give you all the information for the MRI and you can print it from the UM patient portal. See you Friday."

Cheryl didn't get a chance to question further. She would have to wait until Friday to get the rest of the story. She could tell there was more than just the MRI test. She was glad that Alan would be with her.

Early Friday morning. Cheryl got up before Alan and took her shower and did her hair and makeup so she could vacate the bathroom before Alan got up. Shane was already in the kitchen having a bowl of Crunchy Raisin Bran and Cinnamon Toast Crunch cereals mixed together his favorite quick breakfast.

"Good morning Mom. Going to work bright and early?"

"No. I have a doctor's appointment this morning. Dad is going with me. I should find out today what's going on. We should be home early afternoon. What are you up to today? Looks like a nice day out there today."

"I think I'll sit on the deck and read some of the books I ordered from Amazon. Amazing! I should get them today. It's on your charge."

"Sounds like fun. Hope you find out some history behind that coin you found. You're a regular sleuth Son. You don't let go of anything until you finished it. Your father and I are so proud of you. We can discuss what you find when I get home."

Alan came into the kitchen as the conversation was winding down. "What are you two talking about?"

"Just talking about our plans for the day. I told Shane about the doctor appointment today and he is going to do some research on his gold dollar. I'm so glad you're going with me today Alan. I'm a little nervous of what Doctor Hammoud might tell us."

Alan placed his hands around her shoulders and gave her a warm hug. "Don't worry. I know it's easy to say don't worry, but whatever it is we will fix it together." Cheryl dabbed a small tear forming in the corner of her eye.

They parked close to the University of Michigan satellite clinic. It was home to Dr. Hammoud's office and the MRI labs. Cheryl had been there many times for her annual gynecological and breast exams. Alan had rarely been there. He was one of those men who wouldn't start seeing a doctor on a regular basis until something went wrong. It was the attitude that I'm young and healthy or I don't want to know or a combination of both.

They checked in at the front desk with the usual questions from the receptionist: Been out of the country, any cough or cold, etc. etc.? She was given an I-pad with questions regarding her current health and any prescriptions she was currently taking. She flipped through all the screens and checked all the boxes. Cheryl brought one of her crosswords with her and Alan grabbed one of the golf magazines as they waited.

Finally, a wave from the nurse. "Cheryl, the doctor is ready for you."

The nurse weighed her and took her blood pressure, and they were led to one of the economy-size-office-exam rooms, smelling of sweet antiseptic.

"Good morning you two. Glad to see you came along Alan. I requested Cheryl bring you along as a driver but I really had another reason." Cheryl and Alan held their hands tighter as Doctor Hammoud spoke. "Your test for CA125 came back. It's the one for measuring the tumor marker for ovarian cancer." The word "cancer" came out as a shout! Cheryl and Alan flinched and squeezed their hands tighter together. "Normal range for this antigen is zero to 35. Your marker is at 120. Normally anything over 65 is suspect." Both had their ears sensitively tuned to what the doctor was saying but would forget most of it by the time they left the room. Only the words OVARIAN and CANCER would be remembered!

"So, what we will do is to have you take the MRI as planned and that will give us a clear picture if there is indeed an ovarian tumor and what the therapeutic plan will be. I don't want to give you any false hope but, sometimes high CA readings can be a result of pregnancy . . . I'm assuming that's not the case?" Doctor Hammoud forced a smile as did Cheryl and Alan. "Uterine fibroids, benign tumors, cysts and others can also give false positives. Since I'm an oncologist as well as your gynecologist I will be taking care of you through your treatment. If surgery is required, then I will consult with the surgeon as far as treatment. I will refer you to Doctor James Roberts, head of surgical oncology here at the U. I know it's a lot to absorb and I am sorry. Do you have any questions?"

Alan said, "Let's get through the MRI and let this all sink in and I'm sure we'll have many questions. How about you Cheryl. Any Questions?"

Cheryl just shook her bowed head and reached into her purse for a tissue.

The MRI went without any glitches and both Cheryl's and Alan's emotions were starting to calm down. "You want to stop at Big Boy if you're hungry?"

"As a matter of fact, I am hungry despite all of this news. Let's stop and have a nice lunch. I could knock down a Slim Jim and a plate of fries and a strawberry shake. Maybe it'll improve my attitude."

"Can't hurt," Alan said with a smile and another comforting hug.

Shane had settled into one of the brown wicker deck chairs. The books had been delivered. He brought the books, a pen, a marker and a cold bottle of Dasani water in a Corona beer sleeve. He leafed through one book and saw that it was more fiction than fact. The author had taken some of the proven and unproven facts and weaved an interesting story around a Confederate soldier that had stolen some of the gold that was en route to a safe farmstead in the Deep South. He browsed the chapters and decided that fiction for the most part, wouldn't help him much, in searching for something that he might need.

The second book was more of a history book. It had dates, a timeline, maps, key players, photographs and diagrams. Normally reading a history book could be a very dry undertaking for Shane. Although he did enjoy history class in school, sometimes the dryness of it put a wet cloth on it. But this history – maybe because he might have a stake in it – was proving to be one of the most interesting history books he had ever read. After he went through the timeline and the key players listed in the front of the book, he got out his green Sharpie highlighter and went through it page by page. He didn't read every word like reading a novel. He concentrated on the bold section headings and when he saw something that looked like it might specifically reference gold coins, he would read it slowly and mark any interesting facts.

Some of the facts that caught his eye were;

Toward the end of the war in 1865 The Confederate Army was charged with gathering all the gold and moving it to different cities in the South.

There were numerous Confederate soldiers and

some midshipmen (sailors) assigned to move and guard the gold, silver and paper currency.

The treasure was moved from city to city, by train and wagons and back to trains. It was kept in houses and warehouses. It was carried in money belts, shot bags, iron chests, wood boxes and saddlebags.

There was one small paragraph that Shane almost glossed over. It was a quote from a memoir of General Basil Duke, in charge of moving the treasure to Washington Georgia. He stated that when the gold pieces were transferred from a boxcar to a wagon, one of the boxes was found left in one of the corners of the boxcar covered with burlap. It was suspected that one of the Confederate soldiers – with Northern ties – possibly from Michigan – had found the box, emptied some of it and left the rest in the boxcar. That soldier was never seen again after the box was discovered. How much might have been stolen was never determined due to the haphazard record keeping and lack of control of the whole endeavor to keep the treasure from The Union.

This one paragraph lit up Shane's interest like his fluorescent Sharpie! He was trying to keep his delusions of grandeur in check. As he got lost in his thoughts, he heard the screen door slide open.

Shane was pretty good at reading people's faces, especially his parents. He could see the somber look on their faces. It was matching the clouds that rolled in over the lake and turned the lake from blue to grey.

"Hi Shane. Let's go into the kitchen and we'll fill you in on the doctor's appointment we just had," Alan said.

They all filed into the kitchen and took seats around the table. All three had their hands laced and resting on the table.

"The doctor told us that your mother could have ovarian cancer." Shane's mouth was agape. He didn't say anything but continued to listen to his father. "They still need to get results from the MRI test and then Mom's doctor will consult with the surgeon and they will have a plan for the overall treatment . . . if needed. I can't tell you for sure but the worst case will be an operation to remove the tumor – if they find one – and then some rounds of chemotherapy. We'll let you know as soon as we do. We don't want to get ahead of all this. We just want to be prepared and we want you to know what's going on."

"Shane, I want you to be strong through all of this. I know it's shocking but with you and your father here with me – if it is serious – then you and your father can help me kick it. Can you do that for me Shane . . . be strong?

"Of course, Mom." Shane got up from the table and walked over to his mother and gave her a welcomed hug that brought the tears to all of their eyes.

"I'm going to tell you something else that will give the strength I will need through this ordeal. You know that scar you have on your belly? We told you when you asked about it years ago, that it was a birthmark. Well, that wasn't quite accurate. We didn't lie to you. We just stretched the truth a bit. The scar is from surgery that you had when you were one week old. When we brought you home, we noticed very quickly that you weren't pooping. And you seemed to be very irritable. We took you in to the pediatrician and had you checked out. They did some x-rays and found that you had an obstruction in your bowel. Meaning that your bowel had a kink in it. They operated and fixed it. We brought you home and within a few days you were pooping with the best of them. I was never so happy to see someone take a good poop. My point is that if you could fight through all that at one-week-old and overcome it – I can certainly fight through this cancer."

"Wow! That's some story. If that can give you some strength, just thinking about it, then I'm glad to have contributed," Shane said and gave his mother another hug. Alan was listening to the back and forth and he was getting teary eyed. He just listened and didn't say anything. Cheryl had said it all so very well. It also gave him a sense of strength – that he could be strong for Cheryl and help all of them through this.

Dr. Roberts office called two days later. The nurse told Cheryl that surgery would be necessary and that they scheduled it for the following week. She told Cheryl that she would have a consult with Dr. Roberts and Dr. Hammoud the day before the surgery. They would tell her what the prep is before the operation, what the operation would be – exactly – and what the follow up treatment would be after the operation.

The prognosis by Dr. Hammoud was correct. There was a tumor on one of her ovaries. The surgery would be to remove both ovaries and any tissue in the area that showed signs of the metastasizing. After a couple of weeks, when she was comfortably recovered from the surgery, the chemotherapy infusions would start. The chemotherapy regimen would be discussed with her prior to the first infusion.

6

The day of the operation Shane asked his dad if it would be alright if he would go with them.

"Of course, Shane. Mom would love to have you there with us to add to the moral support."

The operation was scheduled for eight o'clock that morning. On the way to the hospital there was an ominous silence. The silence continued through the check in and into the operation preparation room. Dr. Roberts finally arrived. The anesthesiologist stood by his side as they both explained the operation and what to expect. Cheryl was given a sedative prior to their visit so she remained calm as the doctors described the process. Alan and Shane were feeling the anxiety that she wasn't feeling.

Alan and Shane gave Cheryl hugs and kisses and "I love you" and she was moved out of the pre-op room to the operating room. They retreated to the surgical waiting room. Alan brought his iPad and logged in on his VPN to work and scrolled through his e-mails in an effort to try to occupy his mind. Shane brought his two books on the history of Civil War gold and tried to do the same. The wait for news from the operating room was painful. Four hours of sipping cold, stale coffee and warm water and staring at iPad screens and pages from a book finally ended.

Dr. Roberts came into the waiting room, still wearing his scrubs and booties. He asked Alan to follow him into a private consultation room. He asked Shane to remain in the waiting room. The consultation room was tiny with barely enough room for a small table and three chairs.

"The operation went very well Alan. She tolerated the anesthetic very well and is in recovery right now. We had to perform an oophorectomy – remove both ovaries – and some surrounding tissue that exhibited signs of metastasizing. We don't want that to happen, especially to allow any cancer cells to move into her lymphatic system. So, I am going to discuss the findings from the operation with Dr. Hammoud and give her my input as to how aggressive we need to be with the chemotherapy. Do you have any questions for me now, Alan?"

"I do. How long will she be here and when will the treatments start?"

"She's relatively young and strong and tolerated everything – so far – very well. I expect to release her within a few days after we remove the drainage tube. Then she'll have to visit Dr. Hammoud for follow up within a week from that date. We should have a schedule for chemo by then. Stitches from the operation will dissolve and will easily be removed. Anything else?"

"No. I guess that's it for now. Thank you, Doctor." Alan got up and extended his hand. Dr, Roberts shook his hand and placed his other hand on top of Alan's. "I know this is difficult for you and your son. But you guys have got to be strong for her. I have seen my share of ovarian cancer cases and I can say that I am very optimistic with all of the new therapeutic drugs and treatments we have today. I can remember when chemo treatment took three days in a hospital. Today you go to an infusion-suite at the hospital and within three hours you're on your way home with very little, if any, side effects. Just hang in there Alan and don't forget about your boy. Remember he's going through the same anxiety that you are."

"Thanks for all that great advice."

"Both of you can go to the recovery area now and she should be waking shortly. I'll show you the way."

Alan motioned to Shane and they followed Dr. Roberts to the recovery area. There were two rows of beds along either wall with curtains separating the beds. The room was quiet except for whispers and the squeaks of nurse's shoes. Alan motioned for Shane to take the one chair and he stood next to Cheryl. Within a few moments Cheryl started to stir.

"Hi guys. All done I guess?"

"Yep, all done and Dr. Roberts said you did just fine."

One of the nurses heard the voices and came into the cubicle. "I'll have Dr. Roberts' assistant surgeon come over and give you some input as far as the operation and what comes next," the portly nurses said with a pleasant smile and comforting voice.

A much too young, Doogie Howser-looking doctor arrived almost immediately and repeated all of the information that Dr. Roberts had relayed to Alan.

Cheryl had just finished her second chemotherapy and things were going as well as could be expected. She wasn't experiencing any serious side effects. The mild nausea she had was treated with Compazine. She hid most of her other side effects like the nausea, her loss of appetite and mild diarrhea from both Alan and Shane. The side effect lurking on the horizon, that she feared most, would be the loss of her hair. She was not an overly vain person. It was just the fear of the unknown. How would she look? How would Alan react? What would Shane say? These were all questions that were yet to be answered!

It was an ideal summer day living on Lake Bilasaana. Cheryl was on the deck enjoying the slight breeze that was keeping the afternoon heat at bay. She had her laptop on the table and was checking into her work website. She had decided to keep working, listing and selling houses as long as she felt able. Her co-workers supported her by offering help if she ever needed it. Alan and Shane were over-helpful. She had to call them off at times, telling them over and over that she was okay.

Shane came on to the deck, dressed in a bathing suit and a Whitesnake vintage tee shirt and flip flops.

"Hi Mom. Can I get you anything? How are you feeling?"

"I'm fine Shane. You can get me another cold water if you don't mind."

Shane brought out an ice bucket filled with ice and three bottles of water. "At your service Madame."

"What are you up to today Shane on this beautiful day?"

"Thought I'd just laze around. Spend some time with you."

Cheryl turned toward Shane and looked directly into his eyes. "Listen Shane. You and your father are treating me like I'm a porcelain doll. I know I'm a doll . . . but," She smiled at Shane and he smiled back over the seriousness that he knew was coming. "But you guys have got to ease up a little. I want you to get back involved with the quest you started when you found that gold coin. I haven't heard a word about it since this whole cancer thing reared its ugly head. If you really want to help me and make me feel better then you have to go back and do whatever you were doing before. If it's the coin or fishing or hanging with Dennis or whatever. What do you say Son?"

"Me and Dad are just trying to help. Yeah, I guess we are being a little over protective. I promise to back off . . . a little bit anyway."

As they were talking, Cheryl noticed Denny and his twin sister Marlyse walking up the lawn toward the deck. Marlyse was carrying in both hands what looked like a casserole. Marlyse walked gingerly up the stairs, staring at the casserole and the stairs, hoping she wouldn't trip, embarrass herself in front of Shane and ruin everything. Denny was walking behind her hoping he wouldn't have to catch her.

"What have you got there Marlyse?"

"My mother made a casserole she thought you might like. It's a spaghetti salad. It's delicious. You can serve it as a side dish or as a meal." She took off the glass lid and presented the salad to Cheryl. Cheryl looked into the casserole and said, "Looks delicious. It's got my mouth watering. Shane, take it and put it in the fridge. We'll return the dish when we're done. Thank your mother very much for me. She didn't have to, but I do appreciate the thought and the gesture."

Shane returned from putting the casserole in the refrigerator and sat back down at the table. Denny and his sister Marlyse were standing next to the railing. "Sit down you two. Shane, go and get some more water or pop or something."

"We're fine Mrs. Krieger, just had some water. How are you feeling? You look great," Marlyse said.

"I feel pretty good. I've had two treatments so far . . . and four to go. I was just scolding Shane here to get back to doing the things he enjoys. He and his father are hovering over me like buzzards. Did Shane tell you about the gold coin he and Denny found?"

"What gold coin?" Denny said in a startled voice. "You didn't tell me about any gold coins . . . like the ones that we saw fall into the lake when we found the bayonet?"

"Yep. Sorry I forgot to tell you with all that's going on here, Shane glanced at his mother. "I forgot all about it. Let me show you. I'll go get it."

Shane returned within a minute and opened the Altoids box with the 1861 gold coin and handed it to Denny.

"Wow! That is beautiful," Marlyse said as she peeked over Denny's shoulder.

"What are you going to do with it? Did you have it appraised? I get half . . . finder's fee," Denny laughed.

"I've done some research but haven't had time to get it appraised. It's from the Civil War – 1861. Minted by the Confederate Army in Georgia during the War"

All during the conversation Marlyse was staring at Shane. Cheryl noticed and this wasn't the first time she saw Marlyse show her interest in Shane. She would often tag along with Denny when he came over to hang with Shane. Denny didn't notice or give it a second thought. She was his sister – his twin sister – so hanging with him didn't seem that strange. Cheryl's motherly instinct saw the attraction loud and clear. She was wondering when Shane might return the attraction . . . or did he already? She wondered.

Cheryl jumped into the conversation. "Why don't you guys do some searching together? Maybe Marlyse can help. You know women are smarter than men when it comes to searching for things. How about it Marlyse? By the way, I love your name. How did your mom come up with that name? I never heard it before."

"My two aunts are Mary Lou and Elyse, so Marlyse. And Denny – Dennis – was named after her other sister, Denise." Denny smirked. "I would like to help in researching the coin if you guys want."

Denny and Shane looked at Marlyse and they both scratched their chins and let out synchronized hmms.

"I've got a better idea. I already did a lot of research on the coin with my mom and by myself and I don't think there's much to find, but if you want . . . be my guest. I was thinking of the other interest I had. I always wanted to do a good search of Orchard Island and see if I can find the cabin that is supposedly there. My mom did some searching on the history of the property so maybe we could find the cabin? They are going to limit exploring the island when they designate it as a historical site. So, we only have this summer to walk freely there. And who knows what we could find. What do you guys think?"

Cheryl noticed Shane looking directly at Marlyse when he said, "you guys", so maybe the spark was already there? This conversation with Shane and Marlyse and Denny had been a great distraction from her health. She was hoping that Shane would get reengaged with his interest and that would help her sail through the hard times and savor the good times.

"I'm in!" Marlyse was all for it. Denny pursed his lips and shook his head but then replied. "Okay I guess so. When do you want to do this exploring?"

How about . . . not tomorrow . . . but the day after? You guys come over early and we can row out there before the sun gets too hot. Wear some comfy clothes and shoes. I'll bring a map of the island and mark up some areas we can start with."

"Wow, Sak . . . I mean Shane." Denny noticed Cheryl's pout when he called Shane Sak. You're really into this stuff. It might be fun."

Denny and Marlyse left and Cheryl and Shane watched them walk across the lawn next to the lake, back to their house which was a half a block away, on the neighboring cul de sac.

"That Marlyse is a pretty girl Shane, isn't she?"

"Yeah, I guess so,"

"I notice the way she's looking at you. I think she's more interested in exploring a closer relationship with you rather than the island." Cheryl smiled and nodded her head at Shane.

"Mom . . . knock it off. She's just a friend. Let's leave it at that."

Cheryl smiled and knew she hit a soft spot. *The trip in two days could be interesting*, she thought. She went back to her iPad and Shane grabbed a couple of fishing poles, already rigged, and went out to his boat. He hadn't fished in a while and was feeling a little better about his mother's health.

Denny and Marlyse came over two days later. Bright and early. The sun was just starting to light up the sky like a fuzzy soft peach.

"You two sit in the back and I'll row over to the island," Denny offered.

Shane gave Marlyse a hand getting into the boat and followed her to the transom-seat and squeezed in beside her. Their hips comfortably touching. Denny got in, sat down, pushed the small boat away from the dock and began to row. As they approached the island there was an armada of teal ducks silently making their way away from the island. They swerved just a bit to avoid the oncoming vessel.

Denny found the birch tree next to "The Hole" that had become a regular mooring spot. They were all wearing shorts and Crocs water shoes. Denny and Shane stepped into the shallow sandy bottomed shore-line and Shane once again held out his hand and helped Marlyse, out of the boat.

"I mapped out a trail that I think will work. It takes us around the shoreline of the island. The thought is . . . that as we make our way we can look toward the in-terior and see if we spot anything. Sound like a plan?"

"Sounds like a plan, Bwana," Denny quipped.

There was somewhat of a path along the shoreline with minor interruptions where the summer growth had overtaken the quasi-path. Shane found a cane sized branch he was using to beat away some of the taller grasses. They moved slowly and were looking inward

.

in hopes of finding something that would pique their interest. The sameness of grass, weeds, tree limbs and rocks was getting boring. After about an hour, they all spotted it at the same time.

"Hey, look to your left. Looks like a chimney," Shane shouted.

"We see it Shane," Marlyse shouted back.

Shane hurriedly turned left and began to clear a way toward the structure they all spotted. It was about a hundred yards away from the shore. They walked through a bed of burnt-orange oak leaves sprinkled with trillium peeking through, making nature's spring-carpet. Marlyse stepped gingerly, trying to avoid stepping on the white flowers; Shane and Denny paid no attention to where they stepped. As they got closer, they could see the fading remnants of an orchard. When they got closer still, they could see that it was indeed a chimney. It was all that was standing of what appeared to be a log cabin at one time. What had been the walls had all fallen over . . . in the same direction. The wall nearest the lake fell in toward the center of the structure and covered the floor. It was uneven and appeared to have fallen on something. The opposite wall fell outward of the cabin, in the same direction as the other wall. This caused the adjoining wall to collapse downward into the cabin. It was apparent that something powerful like a strong wind off the lake had pushed the walls in. The chimney made of fieldstone withstood whatever knocked the walls in and stood proudly erect with only slight damage.

They walked around looking at where they might get further into the debris. Shane picked up one of the smaller logs from the caved-in wall and peeked under.

"Looks like an old table and chair under here . . . smashed to smithereens. Did anyone bring their phone? We could take some pictures." They both said "No!"

"Okay Shane, you found your cabin. Now what?" Denny asked.

"I'd like to look around some more and see if we can find any artifacts, like food utensils or knives or whatever. Denny, you remember what we found in that knapsack . . . that bayonet. My mom found that the haversack – that's what they called it – was from the Civil War and so was the bayonet. We found that gold coin in the haversack, so maybe they're connected to this place. Just maybe?"

"I'm tired and this pile of logs is not too interesting to me. Let's head back. You guys can come back whenever and dig through this pile of crap," Denny said.

"Shane, I'll come back with you. We could put on some better clothes and boots for rooting around in this stuff and bring our phones and maybe a hammer or shovel, flashlight or whatever. I'm interested!" Marlyse said looking at Shane's eyes.

"Okay. We'll go back. Now that we know where it's located, it'll save us some time. You're right Marlyse, we should dress for the occasion and bring some tools with us. Denny, you're a stick in the mud. Marlyse and I will do some archeology and when we find King Tut's treasure we're going to count you out." They all laughed and started their way back to the boat.

On the way back Shane and Marlyse discussed plans for their next exploration of the cabin on Orchard Island. They decided to return next week. They would dress appropriately. Their list would be: long pants and boots, DEET mosquito repellant, phones, a shovel, a hammer, a flashlight. Denny declined once more and told them to have fun.

That evening at the dinner table Shane told his parents all about their exploration. He told them of finding the blown over cabin and that he and Marlyse were planning on going back next week.

"What about Denny? Isn't he going?" Cheryl asked.

"He's not interested. I guess he doesn't have his sister's inquisitive gene. That's okay. When we find anything of value, we'll only have to split it two ways,"

Shane said with a smile.

Cheryl rolled her eyes with a coy smile on her face.

"You two be careful out there. Make sure you take your phones. Watch out for snakes and other critters and don't do anything dangerous," Alan warned.

They finished their dinner and after they all pitched in cleaning up, they all went out on the deck to enjoy a spectacular evening; watching the sun sink into the lake. Normally Shane would be off and running after dinner; either fishing or riding his bike over to Denny's or hold up in his room playing games on PlayStation. Little League baseball practice would be starting shortly so he knew that would take him away from spending time with his family. Dad or Mom would pick up other friends and drop him off at practice and he would usually find a ride back with one of the other parents. Since Cheryl's health situation came up, he felt that he had to spend as much time as he could with her. He remembered his mother's request to stop hovering, but he still felt a compulsion to take advantage of those moments when they were all together. There would be plenty of time – when her treatments were all over – to spend time with his friends or his other interests.

7

Alan approached Shane the following week and asked him to join him on the deck.

"Shane, I have a favor to ask. Your mother has an infusion treatment this week on Wednesday and I have to be out of town. I have a big corporate dog-and-pony show in Long Beach, and I won't be able to take her for her infusion. I'd like you to go with her, if for nothing else than moral support. She could go by herself, but something may come up where she would be at risk driving back alone. Can you do that for me . . . and for her?"

"Of course, Dad I'll go with her. I have that excursion planned with Marlyse, but I can fix that with her. She won't mind. No big deal."

"Thanks Son."

Alan felt more at ease now that Shane would be going with Cheryl for her treatment and Shane felt warm inside. Warm that he was contributing to helping his mother and warm that it was another chance to spend time with her. He texted and then called Marlyse. She understood completely and they rescheduled their excursion for the following week.

Cheryl was glad that Shane would be taking her for her treatment. It would be a chance for him to see that the infusion was not as bad as it sounded, and it could be quite relaxing for some. She told him that he should bring something to read or have some games on his phone. She would be taking a small clipboard with her crossword puzzles; some magazines and she would pack some sandwiches and treats in a small soft-walled cooler.

The ride to The University of Michigan Cancer building was filled with mostly small talk. They parked in the attached parking structure and made their way up to the third-floor infusion suites. Cheryl checked in and they took a seat next to an aquarium set into a mural wall of characters from *The Little Mermaid*. It was only a matter of minutes before a nurse came out, got their attention, and waved her into the suite.

"Betty, this is my son Shane. Shane this is Betty, one of my infusion nurses. All the nurses here are fantastic. They make this visit as comfortable as possible."

Betty smiled politely. "Handsome young man. Looks like your husband and I can also see some of your good looks in him, especially the hair."

As they passed the coffee room Betty explained to Shane. "This coffee room is for all the patients and caregivers. There's coffee and tea, water and soft drinks, graham crackers, yogurt, ice cream or sherbet and the best . . . Einstein Bros. fresh bagels – as big as your head."

As they entered the main infusion suite area Shane looked around. It wasn't what he expected. There was a line of about fifteen brown leather lounge chairs, mostly occupied, facing the windows looking out onto the hospital quad that resembled a giant arboretum It looked like one of the airport frequent flier exclusive member suites – except for the IV poles standing guard next to each chair.

Shane watched in silence as Betty the IV nurse, set up a bag of Cisplatin chemo on the pole, checked his mother's blood pressure, heart rate and put an oxygen tracker on her finger. Cheryl was used to the routine and wore a short sleeve scoop neck shirt. This allowed the nurse to easily access the infusion port that Cheryl had under her skin near her collar bone.

Betty said, "It'll take about two hours to empty so make yourself at home . . . and Shane don't forget about the coffee room. Cheryl settled right in and began working on her crossword puzzles. Because of the side-effect of the Dramamine, she took to control any nausea, she quickly dozed off into a nap with a soft snore. Shane smiled as he saw the look of contentment on his mother's face. Betty came by to check on the Cisplatin delivery system and smiled as he saw Shane looking lovingly at his mother.

He was getting a little thirsty and hungry, so he peered into the cooler they brought. He didn't see anything enticing so he decided to take a walk over to the coffee room and see what those bagels looked like that the nurse was raving about. The bagels were stored in an over-the-counter glass-doored warming-cabinet – and – Nurse Betty was right. The cabinet was full of shelves of a variety of huge warm bagels

Shane took out an onion sesame topped bagel. It was pre-cut so he opened it up and slathered it with crème cheese and a grabbed a bottle of orange juice. As he was making his way out of the room, looking at the bagel on the paper plate he was holding, he bumped into an IV pole.

"Excuse me," he said and looked down and saw a seven or eight-year-old girl in a flowery hospital gown pushing the pole with the IV tubing leading to a gauze bandage on her forearm. She was wearing a *Little Mermaid* head scarf on her head.

"Hi Mister. Could you get me a chocolate ice cream from the fridge? They're way in the back and I can't reach with this pole."

"Sure. What's your name?"

"It's Chrissy."

Shane opened the small refrigerator and looked inside. There was no ice cream! The top shelf was empty, and the other shelves only had sherbet. His heart dropped.

"I'm sorry Chrissy. There's no chocolate ice cream. There's only sherbet. I could ask the nurse if we could find some somewhere else."

"No. That's okay Mister. Just give me one of the sherberts."

Shane found a chocolate sherbet cup, peeled off the lid, grabbed a plastic spoon and handed it to Chrissy realizing that she was steering the IV pole with one hand and would have to carry the sherbet with the other hand.

"Can I carry it for you or help you with the pole? Where are you going?"

"I'm just going right next door where all the kids are getting their treatments. I think they call it the pederick or something like that. I can make it by myself. Thank you, Mister."

She turned and wheeled the pole with one hand and held the sherbet with the other and Shane watched her leave. Her gown was flapping open showing her *Little Mermaid* panties. His heart was hurting and his eyes were welling up with tears. *Why, why?* He dumped the bagel into the trash.

Cheryl was stirring from her nap and the bag of Cisplatin had flattened out – nearly empty. She noticed Shane's eyes and face and knew that something was bothering him.

"What's the matter Son? Something bothering you?"

"I'm fine. It's just that I ran into a little girl in the coffee room. I guess the pediatric suite is right next door. It broke my heart Mom. It's bad enough for adults to go through this, but a child that doesn't understand why they have to suffer like that . . . the world is not fair, I guess.

The sorrow that was causing her son to feel bad started to wear on her. The IV was removed and they collected all their things and made their way to the elevator.

"Hi Mister. It's me Chrissy. You remember me? I'm going back for another sherbert. I'm glad you got one for me. I really liked it. Thank you," she said and continued to wheel away toward the coffee room.

"You're welcome Chrissy. See you around."

Chrissy waved.

Cheryl just observed.

It was the first time someone called him Mister and it would be an honorific that would stay in his heart forever.

8

After the hospital visit with his mother, Shane called Marlyse and made arrangements to resume their exploration of the cabin on Orchard Island. He told Marlyse to be over early the next day . . . sunrise. He would bring a shovel, a hatchet and a flashlight. He asked her to bring some water and maybe a snack or two. He reminded her to wear long pants, heavy shoes or better yet, boots and don't forget her phone.

Marlyse was at his deck as the sun was pinching its' way over the horizon. Shane had already loaded the boat with a spade-shovel, a small hatchet he had once use at Boy Scout camp, and a police-size Maglite flashlight. He threw in a couple of bottles of water into the haversack that he and Denny found and threw it into the boat with the rest of the supplies.

Marlyse was dressed in tan cargo pants and a Michigan State forest-green sweatshirt. She had her moderate length hair in a short, tight, pony tail and a slight blush of lipstick. Unlike brother Denny's stocky physique, Marlyse's beginnings of a summer tan accentuated her lithe body and good looks. The beauty was not lost on Shane as he saw her approach.

"All ready to go Marlyse?' Shane greeted her.

"I'm ready. Hope we get lucky and find something. I'm kind of excited. How about you Shane?"

"Yeah, I'm ready for some adventure. Let's go."

Shane helped her into the boat and as she seated herself on the transom-seat he handed her the small cooler she brought for the trip. He stepped into the boat with his arms outstretched to keep his balance. Making their way to the island, the sun was halfway up and shining into Marlyse's soft green eyes. As he rowed facing the rear of the boat, he appreciated the striking sun-sparked portrait of Marlyse.

Shane steered the boat near the familiar birch and rowed as far as he could onto the sandy shore. He jumped out of the boat to avoid getting his boots wet and he tied the bow to the birch tree. Marlyse handed him all the equipment and supplies they brought and he helped her take a small jump onto dry land. He was becoming more and more aware of a warm feeling whenever he grabbed her hand to help her in and out of the boat. She was feeling the exact same thing.

"Oh look . . . the turtles." Marlyse said as she pointed to a log half-in and half-out of the water near a willow tree.

Shane turned and saw that the half of the log that was out of the water was lined up with painted turtles and sand turtles. Their shells lit up by the sun looked like army helmets ready for inspection.

They split up the supplies and tools and found the path that they previously used toward the cabin. They had to walk single file on the narrow weed and brush lined path. It only took half the time it took them on their maiden trip to find the cabin. Marlyse had her phone at the ready and took pictures along the way and as they approached the cabin, she took a wide-angle vista shot.

"Let's clear off that fireplace hearth and we can park our stuff there while we search around," Shane said.

Shane stepped gingerly on the logs that he felt were safe and Marlyse followed him until they reached the fireplace. There were a few smaller logs that had fallen on the hearth and Shane grabbed them and threw them aside. They placed their belongings on the hearth and each sat down beside the pile. Marlyse grabbed two bottles of water from the small cooler and offered one to Shane. They sat in silence, getting hydrated and both thinking about their situation. Shane had completely forgot about his trip to the hospital with his mother and his encounter with Chrissy.

"How's your mom doing? You went with her to the hospital, right?"

"I did go. She's doing great. She went through the treatment like a trooper . . . as my dad would say. The worst part was that I met a little girl there that was going through chemo. It was pretty shocking. I guess we never think about little children going through treatment like that. It was just something I never thought about before."

"You sound concerned. Was the little girl going to be okay?"

"I hope so. She seemed pretty strong and was taking it in stride. She didn't complain at all. She was just worried about getting some ice cream. Let's get to work," Shane wanted to end the conversation before he got too sappy.

"I want to see if I can clear the middle over there where I picked up that log and found something the last time we were here. Maybe you can help me?"

They carefully stepped over the fallen logs to the middle of the debris which had a raised section. There was one of the larger logs from the wall on top of the pile. Shane lifted and grunted as he raised it as far as he could. Marlyse tried to help. They got the log almost on end and Shane shoved as hard as he could and the log fell away exposing some smaller logs underneath. They worked together picking up the smaller logs and heaving them away so they could see what was underneath. When they had all the logs cleared, they saw that there was both a handmade table and chair and that both had collapsed under the weight of the logs.

Shane lifted the tabletop on end and flipped it over, exposing the dirt floor area under the table. They were sweating as they tossed around the logs and the sun was heating up the air. Marlyse sat on one of the logs next to the clearing and took out her phone and began to take a picture-show of shots that they could look at later. She started with the clearing they had just made and worked her way around the whole scrambled scene.

While Marlyse was taking pictures, Shane dug around in the cooler and found two PB&J sandwiches. He unwrapped one and offered the other to Marlyse. They ate in silence as they looked around the mess that the blizzard had created many years ago.

"Not much here I guess," Shane said as he sat next to Marlyse on the log. "Maybe . . . let's look around the edges and see if we can see anything else interesting."

Shane got up and tiptoed through the rubble over to the hearth and grabbed the shovel. Marlyse followed. They worked their way around the periphery of the cabin, poking and looking under any log that appeared to be easy to move with the shovel. They continued to walk around the outside of the cabin until they came to the remnants of the orchard.

"Looks like there was some sort of orchard here at

one time. I guess that's why they call it Orchard Island . . . Duh!" Marlyse said and they both smiled at each other and let out a laugh. Marlyse took more pictures.

"Let's call it a day. I'm getting tired and I'm sweating like a pig." Shane lifted his arm and grimaced. "You probably want to stay away from me for now," Shane said.

"I'm sure my deodorant is working overtime also. Yeah, let's head back. Maybe we can come back again . . . once more. What do you think Shane?" Marlyse said hoping he would agree. She liked being with him and if another trip to the island would happen, then she would welcome it.

"I guess we could come back. I'm going to look at that map again and see if there's anything else we can look for. And you took a lot of pics. We can go over them and see if we missed anything. Let's go, *Dora the Explorer*."

Marlyse got a nice warm feeling from Shane's agreeable comments.

That evening after Shane had taken a shower and freshened-up he found his mother sitting on the deck gazing out over the lake. She was wearing a black scoop neck shirt and white shorts. Her laptop and crossword puzzles were sitting idle on the table.

"Did you eat Mom? Where's Dad? On the road again . . . sang Willie Nelson," Shane said with a lilt in his voice.

"Very funny Shane. Yes, Dad's in California again. I'm not very hungry. No appetite."

"I could order a pizza or something if you want."

"You go ahead and order one. My purse is on the kitchen table."

Shane went inside – called Papa Romano's – and ordered a large supreme pizza – to be delivered. He opened his mother's purse and dug out a twenty-dollar bill from her wallet. As he put the wallet back into the purse there was a noticeable amount of blonde hair on the wallet and the outside of the purse.

As he went back out onto the deck his eyes were drawn to his mother's head and to the black shirt. The contrasting blonde hair that fell onto the black shirt was troubling. He saved any comments to himself. He knew what was happening and what the outcome would be.

The pizza came. Cheryl struggled to get most of one piece eaten. Shane tried to lighten the meal as he told his mother of his trip with Marlyse to Orchard Island.

"She took a bunch of pictures. I told her to organize then and put them on her laptop and we can look at them . . . maybe tomorrow. You'll see what the island looks like and what a mess the cabin is. But we didn't find any treasure . . . yet!"

Cheryl listened and tried to show interest as the thought of losing her hair was taking over all of her thoughts.

Alan came back home the following day. Shane was busying himself fishing and texting Marlyse. They had a quiet dinner. Shane saw his – usually enthusiastic mother – now quiet and tired looking.

Alan was also aware that Cheryl was not the same woman he left just a few days ago.

Cheryl excused herself, saying she was tired and was going up to get ready for bed.

Shane went into his room, troubled by his mother's lethargy!

After a few hours, Shane was getting tired of playing and texting on his computer and decided to go downstairs and watch TV. As he passed his parents' bedroom, he heard them talking and he noticed the door was slightly ajar. The voices he heard were strained and sad. He looked through the opening in the doorway and he could see his parents' reflection in the bathroom wall mirror. His mother was sitting on a vanity chair with a towel over her shoulders. His father had scissors in his hands and was holding onto a hank of his mother's golden hair. She was instructing his father how to cut as she looked into the mirror. His father was wiping his eyes in his tee shirt sleeve in between cuts of hair that he was throwing into the waste basket.

Shane was devastated. He went back into his room and laid face down on his bed. All he could do was feel sorrow. He thought about Chrissy and her *Little Mermaid* scarf. He was struggling with what he could do to help his mother. Nothing came to mind. He eventually fell asleep on his moist pillow.

Shane woke up late the next morning. He realized he had fallen asleep in his tee shirt and shorts. As he walked into the hallway, he saw that his parent's bedroom door was open. The bed was made so he assumed his dad had gone to work and his mother was downstairs. An idea had popped into his head — as he looked into the bathroom that was full of sorrow last night.

He went into the cabinet on his father's side of the double sink vanity and retrieved the supplies he needed and headed back to his bathroom.

His mother was sitting on the deck with the back of her scarfed head facing him. He bent down and gave his mother a kiss on the cheek without mentioning the scarf. He went around the other side of the table and sat down facing his mother.

Cheryl didn't know whether to laugh or the cry as Shane slid the red cowboy scarf off of his bald head.

"Shane! What have you done? Oh my God. You shouldn't have done that. All your beautiful hair!"

Shane got up and walked over to his mother as she stood up. They embraced and felt the motherly love melting between them.

"I just wanted you to know that we are all in this together. It'll grow back just like yours will. Maybe we can have a contest as to who's will grow faster?" Cheryl smiled as she wiped away a tear.

"So, Mom . . . I'm going to call Marlyse and if she has all the pictures from the island ready . . . I'm going to ask her over and we can give you a slideshow. You okay with that?"

"Of course. I would love to see them . . . and Marlyse. She's such a pretty girl and so much of a pleasure to be around. You agree?"

"I do Mom."

You are such a comfort to me Shane. And, you really didn't have to shave your head, but I do appreciate it. Another thing you should know. The chemo

— although it is working and my CA125 cancer markers are going down — it is taking a toll on other parts of my body — like the hair and my appetite, my energy. What I'm trying to say is that my blood, the white cells, are going down and that's not a good thing. The drug they're giving me, Cisplatin, doesn't discriminate. It attacks the cancer along with any quick growing cells like hair and stomach lining and blood. So, after all my future treatments, your father will have to give me an injection of Neupogen on the day following my infusion. It helps to keep the white blood cell count up. If that goes too low, I won't be able to get an infusion and might even need a transfusion. Enough of that! I just wanted you to know what's going on. As you said, we're all in this together!"

"Thanks for sharing Mom. How about some breakfast? I can make scrambled eggs."

"As a matter of fact, I am feeling a little hungry. You make the eggs and I'll take care of the rest." They enjoyed a breakfast together and Cheryl enjoyed eating for the first time in a while.

9

S hane called Marlyse and asked her if she had the slideshow of the island pictures ready. She anxiously answered. "I am ready. Can I come over now or a little later?"

"Why don't you plan for about two hours from now? I want my mother to join us and she's about to take a nap. Okay?'

"Okay. I'll see you in two."

Cheryl enjoyed her one-hour nap and felt refreshed and mentally better after her breakfast with Shane and knowing that Marlyse was coming over and they were going to share some pictures from their excursion of the island.

Shane waited on the deck while his mother freshened up from her nap. She stared in the mirror as she re-folded and put on her paisley green scarf. She thought about what Shane had done by shaving his head and she felt warm inside.

Shane saw Marlyse approaching. She was dressed in white cut off shorts, white Sketcher slip-ons and a

Pink World Tour tee shirt. He tried not to stare but the 'sister of a friend' category for Marlyse was fading into a girl that he wanted to be with.

Marlyse's jaw dropped and her fingers went to her lips as she saw Shane's bald head. She had the same reaction as Cheryl did. She didn't know whether to laugh or to cry.

"What did you do Shane? OMG! Your beautiful hair." As she was exclaiming, she realized why he had shaved his head . . . for his mother.

"What a hero you are Shane." Shane blushed and didn't know what to say.

"Where are we going to do this? Inside might be better to see than here on the deck," was all he could think of. He grabbed his red cowboy scarf and slipped it onto his head and followed Marlyse into the house.

"Hi Marlyse. How do you like baldy here? I'm losing mine so he didn't want to be outdone. I'm starting to feel okay with it. It does have some advantages. Don't have to worry about shampooing and setting and hair appointments . . . and I've read in one of the brochures from the hospital that regrowth of hair after chemo is usually fuller and curlier. My poker straight hair could use a wave or two. Enough of that. I'm anxious to see your slideshow."

"I just have to say that you two are so brave in the way you're handling all of this," Marlyse said.

They all sat on one side of the kitchen table with Marlyse in the middle bringing up the Google slide-show and setting it to change every five seconds.

The first ten pictures were of Shane rowing the boat, their equipment and their approach to the island. Marlyse had a stunning picture of the squad of turtles lined up on the half-submerged log.

"Oh, how cute is that," Cheryl said holding her fingers to her mouth.

The slides continued flicking every five seconds. The next batch of slides was of the path they took to the cabin, the trillium poking through the oak leaves, the grass and weeds, and toppled-over dying or dead trees. A far-off vista of the chimney sticking up on the horizon was the introductory slide to the cabin. Most of the slides of the cabin were mostly the same . . . a jumble of logs like a giant game of Pick-up sticks.

Marlyse had taken three pictures of the clear dirt floor under the table that Shane had flipped over. After the third slide . . . Cheryl shouted, "Wait! Stop! Go back to the last slide. I think I saw something there."

Marlyse hit the back arrow and the pause button and they all stared at the picture of dirt.

"Can you enlarge?" Cheryl asked.

Marlyse placed her thumb and forefinger on the touch screen and spread them giving a closer view.

"Do you see what I see or am I seeing things. There

. . . in the corner. It looks like a glint of something."

Both Shane and Marlyse leaned forward. Shane could smell the faint perfume smell on Marlyse's shirt. They stared for a moment. Shane wanted to hold this position for a bit longer.

"It could be something. I don't know," Shane said. What do you think Marlyse?"

"I don't know. It sure looks like a little fleck of gold or something. But I don't remember seeing anything when we were there?'

"Okay Marlyse. Now back off the picture to the full view. Can you increase the contrast?"

"I think so." She hit the crop button and slid the arrow further to the right and the picture showed more detail as the contrast increased. In addition to the gold fleck taking on more detail, there appeared to be footprints that were showing now.

"Do you guys see the footprints? Or am I imagining again?"

"No, I think there are footprints but that's not unusual. This spot was under a table so footprints could be expected."

"Let's finish the show and then we can come back to this one," Marlyse said.

There were only a few more slides of the cabin and the remnants of the orchard and their trip back to shore. Marlyse reversed the show and went back to the dirt floor slide.

"Maybe it's a mate for your other coin Shane?" Cheryl said.

"Maybe? I guess we'll have to go back again like you said Marlyse when we left." Shane said.

"Can't wait. When do you want to go?" Marlyse responded almost before Shane was through asking.

"Maybe next week. Let me think."

"About time for a break and some refreshments," Cheryl said.

They all got some water and pop from the refrigerator and Cheryl revealed a plate of chocolate chip cookies she made last night after Alan cut her hair and she was looking for something to soften the blow. They sat on the deck under the umbrella-table and Shane brought out the 1861-D gold coin in the Altoids tin. They passed it around the table, felt it and stared at it. They all wondered what was yet to come?

Shane and Marlyse agreed to go back to the cabin in two days. They went over what to bring to help in their search. It was basically the same equipment they brought the last time except Shane had found an old entrenching tool that his grandfather had brought back with him from the Army. It was basically a short-handled fold up shovel that could easily be carried with a backpack.

The day they picked was going to be a hot one – probably in the 80's. They got a late start because Marlyse had an early morning babysitting job she committed to. Because of the weather they were both dressed in shorts, water Crocs and tee shirts. Shane was wearing an Eminem Lose Yourself tee and Marlyse was wearing a vintage Heart tee.

They started to develop a routine; Load the boat, help Marlyse into the boat, Shane row to the mooring birch tree, Marlyse hand all the gear to Shane and proceed to the cabin.

They made their way across the fallen logs, knowing which ones were stable and which weren't. They dropped their gear on the fireplace hearth and Shane said. "Okay Marlyse, let's go and see what we can find. Keep your phone handy to add to your photo parade and . . . be careful walking on these logs."

Shane led the way to the overturned table top and stretched out his hand to steady Marlyse until she got on firm ground. "Let's look at that pic on your phone and see where the gold fleck was on that one shot."

Marlyse opened her phone and began scrolling through her photos. When she reached the one of the dirt floor, she held it so Shane could see it. "I think this was the one," Marlyse said.

Shane took the phone, looked at the photo and looked down at the cleared dirt floor. "It looks like it's up in that corner. Can you see it?"

Marlyse knelt down and reached to the far edge of the clearing and brushed aside some dirt. She found the gold glint and it was indeed another coin! She picked it up with her thumb and index finger and stood back up. She handed the coin to Shane, as she brushed the dirt from her knees, without saying a word. Shane took the coin and brought it up to his face and carefully looked at both sides of the coin. Without thinking or saying anything they reached out – Shane still holding the coin – and they embraced. It was an embrace of discovery – not the discovery of the coin – but the discovery of each other's embrace!

"This is exactly the same as the other coin Marlyse. It even has that D for the Dahlonega Mint."

They sat on one of the logs on the edge of the cleared area and looked at each other with smiles spreading across both of their faces. When the excitement had ebbed a bit, they both were staring down at the dirt floor. "Do you see what I see?" Shane asked.

"I do see some faint footprints like we saw in the picture."

"Not that. I see the footprints too. I'm talking about the faint lines that seem to go around the edges of this clearing. Like there's something under this dirt."

"Yeah, you're right Shane. I do see what you're talking about."

Shane stood up and took out his red scaled Swiss Army Knife from his pocket and opened the largest blade. He knelt down and started to probe at the depressions in the dirt and the blade hit something solid. He started to push the dirt with his hands and Marlyse knelt down and joined him. Within a few minutes they had uncovered the entire area – showing what appeared to be a wooden trap door.

Shane tried to get a grip on the wood but it was wedged-in too tightly from years of weather and the weight of the logs they had removed. He got up and quickly made his way back to their gear and grabbed the entrenching tool. He unscrewed the bezel that held the shovel folded, unfolded it, and retightened the bezel and Voila – a miniature shovel!

Shane pushed the tip of the blade into one of the edges of the wood. He pulled it backward with no results. He pounded with his fist on the end of the shovel to drive it a little more into the opening and again pulled back on the handle. This time the wood started to give and he increased the pressure until the wood rose enough for him to get a grip on the edge. He removed the shovel and handed it to Marlyse. He lifted the wood and flipped it over away from the opening. A whiff of cool damp air rose out of the opening. It felt good on their perspiring bodies.

"Wow. Some kind of cellar, I guess. Hand me the flashlight Marlyse."

"Did you bring one? I didn't see one."

"Oh shit. Woops sorry. I forgot. Let me have your phone. It has a light . . . right?

"Yes sir. Here you go."

Shane took the phone with the flashlight that Marlyse had already turned on. He peered down into the hole and saw that there was a makeshift ladder with three foot-steps. He gingerly stepped down on the first step and gradually eased all of his weight on the step – hoping it would hold him. It did. He stepped down onto the dirt floor. He couldn't stand up straight, so he got on his knees and swept the flashlight across entire perimeter of the cellar. All he could see was a dirt floor and two tan and brown covered crock pots against one of the fieldstone walls.

"What do you see Shane? Anything?"

"Just a lot of dirt and some . . . looks like crocks. I'm going to crawl around and take some pics."

Shane got on his knees and started to crawl around the dark, damp cellar. The damp earth smell was overwhelming but the coolness felt good on his skin. As he crawled around, his bare knees would hit the occasional pebble on the otherwise smooth dirt. He would wince and move on. He made his way over to the crocks against the wall and removed the tops. He held the flashlight over the crocks and peered inside. All he could see were some undistinguishable pieces of mummified fruits or vegetables. He winced from the smell and recovered the crocks and as he did, he noticed the imprint next to the two crocks of what may have been a third crock. He took a picture. He took out the Swiss Army knife and opened up the 2 ½" blade and started to poke it into the soft moist dirt as he made his way around the walls of the cellar. He was hoping to find something buried. His back was getting tired and his knees were getting sore from kneeling on the dirt and pebbles.

"I'm done here," Shane said as he handed the phone up to Marlyse.

"Did you find anything beside the crocks?"

"Nope. But it looks like there was a third crock at one time. I poked around with my knife but didn't find anything."

Shane climbed up the ladder and sat on the log next to Marlyse. She reached over and brushed the moist dirt that was stuck to Shane's knees.

Shane was catching his breath after his jaunt around the fruit cellar. "Oh, thanks for cleaning off my dirty knees," Shane said and looked into her eyes.

"What now Shane? Are we through here?"

"I had a thought. If I remember correctly, your

brother had a Mickey Mouse metal detector at one time. Do you know if he still has it?"

"It might be in the garage. I do remember he got it for Christmas a few years ago. Like everything else he does, his interest faded quickly in metal detecting after a few days searching the beaches and only finding some pennies and a cheap ring. I think he found one of my mother's earing-backs when she lost it outside . . . not sure? He's not like you Shane. You really finish stuff you start. Let's go back and I'll look in the garage and see if I can find it. My dad is a pack rat when it comes to the garage. So that might be a good thing. Stuff in the garage has been there since we moved in. Nothing gets thrown away.

They collected their equipment and headed back to the boat and back to Shane's house.

When Marlyse got back home she found Denny in his room playing *Call of Duty* on his PlayStation.

"Denny, my Dear Brother. I need that metal detector you got for Christmas a couple of years ago. Do you know where it is?"

"Yeah. It's probably still in the garage. If Dad didn't throw it out . . . not likely. Look on the shelves out there. If it's there, you'll need bats. What do you need that for?" Denny said without lifting his eyes from the PlayStation screen.

"Shane and I are doing some exploring in that old cabin. We found a fruit cellar and another coin. We're going to give it a sweep with your detector if it's working."

"Are you sure you're just exploring the cabin . . . you two?"

"Knock it off shithead!"

Marlyse turned around and left Denny to his PlayStation games. She went directly to the garage and after a half-hour of searching she found the metal detector, which was wedged behind one of the shelves. It was a National Geographic Junior, Adjustable, Metal Detector. It was barely 3 feet long – perfect for tight spaces. She flicked on the switch . . . nothing! She found the battery compartment, slid it open and carefully removed 3 lightly corroded AA batteries. She hunted around her father's seldom-used workbench and found a shoe box full of batteries. Luckily there was an unopened package of Energizer AA batteries with a sunglass clad bunny smiling at her. She inserted fresh batteries, turned on the detector and threw a couple of bolts on the lawn. She walked over to where she threw them and tested the detector. Beep! Beep! It worked! She found all the bolts and threw them back on the workbench.

She put on a fresh Katy Perry tee shirt, a spritz

of her mother's Shalimar perfume, grabbed the metal detector and rode her bike back to Shane's house.

Shane was on the deck with his mother. He was showing her the latest 1861-D gold coin that he and Marlyse had found.

"You guys are becoming regular Indiana Joneses," Cheryl said as Marlyse approached the deck. "What have you got there?"

"It's my brother's old metal detector. We're going to use it in that old cellar we found. Did you tell your mother about the cellar?"

"I did. Does that thing work?"

"It does. Why don't you try it? I'll put that coin in the lawn and see if you can find it. Turn your back."

Marlyse took the gold coin and walked a few feet away from the deck and carefully placed the gold coin into a tuft of grass. "Okay turn around and start your search."

Shane could see the gold flickering in the sun but he played dumb and started sweeping the detector away from the coin and slowly worked his way over to the coin waiting for a beep. It beeped and all three of them smiled. Marlyse gave Shane a high-five. Cheryl gave Marlyse a high-five

"Why don't we go back tomorrow? I'm beat and I need a shower if you haven't noticed?" Shane had noticed that his mother was really showing her weakness and her usually rosy complexion was showing a worrisome pale. Tomorrow was Saturday and his father would be home and he wouldn't have to worry about leaving his mother alone.

Marlyse was a bit disappointed that they weren't going back today, but she agreed on tomorrow to resume their search with the detector. Cheryl was glad that Shane was staying home with her.

"Why don't you guys order a pizza or something? I don't feel much like cooking." Even Marlyse could see the feebleness in Cheryl's demeanor!

10

They met early the next morning as planned. Shane had the boat loaded and was sitting on the deck getting familiar with the toy-like metal detector. *Not much to it*, he thought. As he was playing with the detector Marlyse appeared out of the corner of his eye.

"All set Indiana Jones?" Marlyse's voice interrupted his thoughts.

Shane smiled. "I'm ready. Let's go."

They were both excited for two reasons. The thought of possibly finding more gold and the pleasure that they would – spend the day together. There was a slight breeze wafting across the lake and producing sparkling sunlit diamonds. The bow of the boat sliced silently through the ruffled diamond blanket. In addition to their regular equipment Marlyse had packed PB&J sandwiches, a few Dr. Peppers and water. The sun beating down on the lake told them that it was going to be another hot day. They were both dressed in tees. Marlyse was wearing short cargo pants – to

Shane's liking. Shane was wearing long pants, remembering the toll his knees took on their last expedition.

They were both anxious to get the metal detecting under way so they didn't waste any time. They went through their regular routine with the boat mooring and carrying the equipment to the hearth. Shane carried the metal detector and as they walked, he was getting use to the strap and the on-off switch and how to adjust the length. He adjusted the length down to 24" so he would be able to maneuver it in the confines of the cellar.

Marlyse sat on the log next to the cellar trap door. She had her elbows on her knees and her fingers laced as she watched Shane lift the door and flip it over.

"You look like you're praying. You praying for a good find?"

"That and that you don't hurt yourself down there. Be careful."

"I will. Here goes." Shane said as he placed his foot on the first step. He still felt a little unsure of the ladder so he slowly stepped down onto the dirt floor and felt a little safer as he did. He got on his knees and steadied the detector with the strap around his arm and started across the floor to the far wall. He had been thinking about the best way to approach the search.

"Marlyse, can you sit on the edge and shine your phone down here the best you can. It's pretty dark. I should have brought a lantern flashlight."

Marlyse sat on the top of the opening with her feet on the first step. She turned on her phone light and held it down between her legs.

"Yeah, that's a lot better. I can see pretty good now. Thanks."

He started to sweep the detector in one corner and followed the wall to the opposite corner. When he reached the other corner, he brought the 7" head down a little and moved on back to the other corner. When he was about half way through the area, he stopped and turned and looked at Marlyse's legs with the flashlight between them . . . trying to concentrate on what he was saying.

"I need a break. I'm coming up. I'll mark where I left off and come back down."

They sat on the log next to the opening. They were getting use to the damp smell of wood and dirt as it drifted up through the opening. Marlyse opened the cooler and got out two pops and the two PB&J sandwiches. Shane was wiping his forehead and face with his tee shirt. Even though the cellar was relatively cool, the exertion of kneeling, crawling and holding the detector was exhausting.

They ate in silence and Shane was getting his strength back. He was also feeling a little conflicted. He was disappointed he hadn't found anything and was still excited about continuing the search.

"Is there anything else I can do besides hold the light for you? I feel kind of dumb."

"No. You're doing fine. That light is very helpful. Here we go again. Wish me luck."

Marlyse patted Shane on the shoulder and said, "Good Luck. I know if there's anything down there, you'll find it."

Shane crawled down the steps again and was startled by a little creak on the last step. He got back to the middle of the cellar as Marlyse got back on the step with her phone light. He found the line in the dirt where he had left off and he continued his slow methodical sweep from side to side.

He finished sweeping the entire space. His confliction was quickly shifting from excitement to one of disappointment. As he got to the ladder, he looked up at Marlyse.

"Sorry girl. Struck out! I guess there was nothing here to find."

Marlyse looked down and the light from the phone illuminated the dejected look on Shane's face. "I'm sorry and I'm just as disappointed as you are. Oh well, it was fun while it lasted. Let me get out of your way so you can get up here and I'll get you something to drink."

As Marlyse got up and reached over for the cooler

she heard a loud crunch. She turned and peered down the opening. She could see that the step on the bottom of the ladder had broken and Shane was staring at it.

"You Okay? I heard the wood break."

"I'm okay. Better than okay. Look down here."

As the rotted wood step snapped from Shane's weight, it dug into the dirt below and gouged a size-able hole into the dirt. It exposed the top of the third crock, directly under the ladder. Shane knelt down, pulled out his Swiss Army knife and furiously started to dig around the crock. When he had cleared the pe-rimeter down to the bottom, he reached down and carefully lifted the round, 7 ½" high x 4" wide, crock and handed it to Marlyse. Marlyse put her hand around the crock and kept her little fingers underneath the bottom . . . afraid she might drop it!

Shane boosted himself out of the cellar over the broken ladder and sat on the log next to Marlyse. She had placed the crock on the dirt without opening it. It was sitting between their feet.

" Okay Marlyse, you do the honors."

"You sure? It's your find. You should open it." She saw the smile on Shane's face. "Okay if you insist." She carefully lifted the cover that had held its' secret for over 150 years.

The treasure they had been talking about and dreaming about and wondering about was now in front of their eyes. Shane reached into the crock and scooped up a handful of coins and stood up. Marlyse did the same. Shane bent over and let the coins in his hand dribble back into the crock. Marlyse followed suit. As she stood up, Shane grabbed her shoulders and brought her close to him. As if they had rehearsed it – their lips met, their bodies touched and the thrill of discoveries was heightened beyond what they could have imagined. It was a firm but gentle kiss and embrace. Their arms wrapped around each other's waist. They slowly parted, wanting to keep the feeling of the enraptured virgin kiss. Nothing needed to be said. The smiles and looks on their faces said it all. They were both feeling the same ineffable feeling. There were no "sorrys" or apologies. They knew that that kiss and the thrill of discovery would be with them for a long time. No matter what the rest of their lives would bring.

Alan was sitting on the deck reading the Thursday *Milford Times*. He saw Shane and Marlyse approaching in Shane's boat. He was thinking how nice the boat looked gliding across the lake. The sun had just passed the summer solstice and the slight breeze felt refreshing. He went back to reading until he noticed the boat next to the dock and Shane and Marlyse were approaching the house. He noticed that Marlyse was carrying something heavy with a broad smile on her face.

"Boy you're some gentleman. Making Marlyse carry whatever that heavy thing is."

"You'll see why in a minute. Where's Mom? We need her out here for the big reveal."

"She's been feeling tired this morning and she's taking a nap. You know how tired she's been lately with all the chemo side effects. She's been sleeping a couple hours. I guess I could wake her if it's that important."

"It is Dad. You'll see. And I think she will be happy to see what we have. Marlyse, text your brother and tell him to get over here . . . pronto."

Alan went into the house and in a few minutes he and Cheryl came out onto the deck. Cheryl still appearing sleepy-eyed and adjusting her head-scarf as she forced a smile and greeted Shane and Marlyse. "Hi kids. What's so darn important that you had to interrupt my beauty sleep? Just kidding. I was up and getting ready to come down and sit on the deck on this beautiful day." Denny showed up as Cheryl was talking.

"We did it Mom," Shane said as Marlyse set the crock on the patio table. "Show'em what we found Marlyse."

Marlyse carefully, slowly and dramatically re-moved the cover from the crock and tipped it slightly so that Alan, Cheryl and Denny, who were seated next to each other across the table, could see the gold coins filling the inside. Their expressions were the same; eyes wide, mouth agape and saying, "Oh my God" at the same time.

"I knew if there was a treasure out there that you would find it Shane. And you . . . Marlyse, you gave him that extra incentive to keep at it. What now?" Cheryl asked.

"I don't know. What do all of you think?" Shane asked.

Denny chimed in. "Let's see what you've got first. Bring'em out and spread them on the table here." Cheryl reached for a purple Myrtle Beach souvenir beach towel on the back of one of the chairs and spread it on the table.

All five of them took out one coin at a time and lined them up on the towel. The contrast of the gold was striking and appropriate against the regal purple towel. Alan lined them up and had all the heads-side of the coins showing. There was a total of 28 coins – not counting the two they found previously!

"Shane, go get the other coins you found." As Shane was retrieving the coins Alan and Denny turned over the coins showing the tails side of the coins. Shane handed one of the coins to his father. Alan looked at the coin and then looked slowly and carefully at the coins lined up on the towel.

As Alan was looking over the display he said. "Looks like they're all the same – even down to the D mint mark. I'm no numismatist but I would say that they are all in proof condition, or maybe even uncirculated condition. You two have found yourselves a little fortune here. If each one is worth . . . say one thousand dollars, then you're looking at thirty thousand dollars. Good start for a college fund I would say."

"Hey? What about me? You and I found the original coin Shane." Denny pouted.

"Don't worry Denny. You're an equal-share partner in all of this. By the way, your metal detector sucks! We found this crock by accident when the ladder down to the fruit cellar broke. But that's a story for another day." Denny smiled a very contented smile.

As Alan was talking, Cheryl went back into the house. Everyone thought she was getting sick from the chemotherapy treatment that morning. She returned in a few minutes holding an antique-ebony-wood cigar humidor. She placed it on the table next to the gold coins and opened it. There was a smattering of tarnished silver coins along with a few copper pennies. And the slight smell of cherry pipe tobacco.

"This was my father's . . . your grandfather Shane.

It's his old humidor and a bunch of old coins – silver dollars, half dollars, quarters, nickels and dimes, even some V nickels. I don't know if they're worth anything but here's a suggestion – just a suggestion; you three do whatever you think is right. But I would take one of the dollars and mark it in a very inconspicuous way. Say just a tiny pin prick with one of your father's punches. I would put the coin in with these and take it to a dealer and have him, or her, give you an appraisal of the coins and what they would give you for them. When it comes to money, especially something like this that could be worth a lot, you have to be careful in who you trust. What do you think?"

"That's a great plan,' Alan said.

"We . . . Marlyse, Denny and me, haven't really discussed what to do. I guess your plan is as good as any."

"I would take picture of all the coins here including the old silver and make an inventory of the coins in the cigar box: type of coin, date, condition, etc. If we take it into a coin dealer and he sees we have pictures and an inventory, he would be less likely to pull off any funny stuff. Right?" Shane asked rhetorically.

"This calls for a celebration . . . Marlyse, Denny . . . get your folks over here and we'll get a few pizzas and have a nice meal. I'm hungry for a change . . . with all this excitement," Cheryl said.

"One more thing folks. I think it would be a good idea to keep all of this strictly between the family members. I don't think it would be wise to let any of your high-school buddies know about this just yet . . . until you know what you're going to do," Alan cautioned. The three of them nodded their heads.

After a nice meal of salad, bread sticks and fully loaded pizzas and excited-talk about the found treasure, Denny, Marlyse and their parents left. The sun was setting and spreading a congratulatory golden splash across Lake Bilasaana.

Cheryl had cut up 30 pieces of felt so Shane could wrap the coins and prevent them from getting scratched. She did this after Alan had told them that even the slightest scratch on a mint or uncirculated coin would take away from its value. He also wanted to keep Cheryl engaged in the process. He saw that her enthusiasm in her son's treasure was keeping her mind busy and off of her health problems. As her health worsened and the after-effects of the chemo infusions became more evident, he began to worry more. The treasure find was also a way to keep himself from worrying. He didn't want his deep concern to start showing. His goal was to keep their family as normal as possible for as long as possible. He knew that Shane was worried about his mother and that was to be expected. He just didn't want Shane starting to worry about him also!

Alan had a talent for compartmentalizing his life. His work was one compartment. His family life was another compartment. And now he had to open up a new compartment. When Cheryl was napping and Shane was off fishing or spending time with his friends – and Marlyse – Alan would spend his time alone on the deck in these warm months. He would light up one of his cigars – his only vice – and think about Cheryl and what she was going through. He would think about Shane and what he might be going through. He appreciated that Shane had an inordinately close bond to his mother.

By keeping his feelings in check, he could keep his inner emotions to himself and not burden Cheryl or Shane with what he was suffering. To see his wife going through the chemo infusions and more than that – the loss of her hair and the loss of her vim was something he just had to accept and try as best he could to be supportive.

Prayer was something he never thought a lot about. His family was regular church goers at Saint Mary, Our Lady of the Snows in Milford, but it wasn't any more than a routine and a chance to spend some time together and have a nice meal after Mass. On the deck with the relaxing cigar gave him pause and he

started to pray. Prayers to God and saints and whoever would listen, to help them through this trying
time. He knew they were a fortunate family in many
ways but now that good fortune was put aside and he
prayed for Cheryl to make it through and recover so
that that blessed life they shared would return.

On some occasions when Cheryl was having a par-
ticularly hard day, it would bring him close to tears
with the thought that he could lose her. He kept these
thoughts and his feelings private and continued to
show strength in front of Cheryl and Shane.

Shane carefully wrapped each coin after going over
them with a magnifying glass he had used in a long-ne-
glected stamp collection. His un-trained eyes couldn't
find any scratches or other obvious mars on the coins.
He placed them in his grandfather's antique cigar humidor. He asked his father if there was somewhere
safe, he could keep the coins for the time being. He
knew that there was a safe somewhere in the house but
he didn't know where.

"Dad, do you have a place I can keep these coins
until I know what we're going to do with them."

"Of course. We have a safe in our bathroom.
Come on. Bring the coins and I'll show you."

Shane followed his father into the master

bathroom. Alan bent down in between the double sink vanity. He pushed on the panel between the cabinets and the push-open latch snapped the panel open. Inside was a small safe with a digital key pad for the combination. Alan punched in the number and opened the safe. Inside was a bank fire-proof box with all the family documents that needed to be kept safe. Alan's small Kimber 9mm pistol was also in the safe along with an empty shelf.

"Let's see that box Shane." Shane handed the box to his father and Alan slid it onto the shelf. "Perfect. Like it was made for this treasure box."

"The combo for the safe is your mother's birthday and year. 10-21-19-82. got it?"

"Yeah, I got it. Thanks Dad."

"One more thing. The gun is unloaded. I keep a loaded magazine in our closet – just in case. One of these days I'll show you how to use it if you're interested, we can go to the gun range. If not . . . that's okay."

"I'll pass for now."

Now that he had the gold coins safely put away; the next chore was to sort out all of the silver that he put into one of Alan's old Macanudo cigar boxes, make a list by denomination and year, take pictures of each coin, and mark the gold coin he would mix in with the silver coins. He asked Marlyse to help him with that – another lame excuse to spend some time together.

Shane and Marlyse set up Shane's laptop on the kitchen table. They lined up all the silver and copper coins on the table, by denomination and by year. Marlyse was pretty handy with Excel spreadsheets so she took charge and set one up called "Silver threads amongst the Gold."

She set up columns for dollars, half-dollars, quarters, dimes, nickels and pennies. The years covered from an 1890 Morgan Silver dollar to a 1943 steel penny.

Shane called out the coin denominations and their year and Marlyse entered them into the spreadsheet. They took pictures of each of the coins separately and a picture of the coins of each denomination. She added Shane's name and phone number at the bottom of the sheet. When they were through, they put the coins back into the Macanudo cigar box that Shane found in the garage – including the 1861-D gold dollar. Before they put the gold coin in the box, Shane brought in a center-punch and a tack hammer. They studied the gold coin with a magnifying glass on both sides looking for the most inconspicuous spot to mark the coin.

"I think a very slight tap of the punch right here

close to the wreath," Shane said and pointed with the punch to the spot he found.

"Looks good to me. Pretty busy area so a tiny spot should blend in with the wreath."

Shane carefully placed the point of the punch close to the wreath on the tail side of the coin and gave it a healthy strike. He grabbed the magnifying glass and took a look.

"Looks good to me. Have a look Marlyse."

"Okay, now we need a couple of pics of the coin, both sides and a close up of the mark we made. We'll keep these photos out of the box. We'll put copies of your Excel and the pics of the other coins in the cigar box. Now we need to search for a dealer."

They went out onto the deck with a couple of Vernors ginger ales and talked over their next moves. They agreed that they would find a reputable deal-er on line, do some vetting like BBB and any coin associations, etc. If they could find one within biking distance, they would go by themselves. If the dealer was further away, they would have to get Alan to drive them.

"Sounds like a plan. I brought my laptop so we can both search for a dealer . . . might be faster?"

They went back inside and sat across from each other at the table and started their search. When one of them found something, they would alert the other and they would look at the website together. They both enjoyed the nearness while looking over each other's shoulder. After an hour or so of searching the web they finally agreed on a dealer they found in the Novi shopping area. It was called Pot o'Gold. It was in a mini-mall on Grand River Avenue. They would need a ride.

Just as they finished finding the dealer Alan and Cheryl came downstairs. Alan was spending a lot of time working from home so he could help Cheryl with doctors' visits and just to give her support where needed.

"What are you guys up to? You got the coins all organized?" Alan asked.

"Sure do. And we found a dealer over in Novi. We were wondering if you could give us a ride over when you have some time. I know you're busy so no hurry – whenever," Shane said.

"We've got an infusion appointment tomorrow. Getting close to the end of the visits so we don't want to miss any. I could take you after the appointment if everything goes well as I expect it to."

"I should be okay. We'll pick you up after we get back. Should be late morning. Will that work?" Cheryl added.

"That'll be great. Thanks." Marlyse said.

The following day was bright and sunny. The temperature was going to be a pleasant 80 degrees. Marlyse came over to Shane's mid-morning and they sat of the deck with the cigar box full of coins waiting for Alan and Cheryl to return from the hospital. Both were silently hoping first of all that the treatment went well and then, that they could get to the dealers and get the ball rolling on the coins and specifically – the 1861-D gold dollar.

As they were discussing and going over the photos and the Excel spreadsheet and the photos of the coin; Alan and Cheryl came out onto the deck.

"You treasure hunters ready? We can leave now if you're ready," Alan said.

"We're ready. How did the treatment go? You doing okay Mom?"

"I'm fine. Getting used to the routine. Not as

many side effects now. I see your hair is starting to grow back Shane. So is mine. Got a little curl in it too. Can't wait till I can style it. Okay let's go."

They all got into Alan's Explorer, Shane and Marlyse in the back and Cheryl riding shotgun. The drive down to the dealers was about a half an hour. The strip mall was located on Grand River, just south of The Twelve Oaks Mall.

The coin dealer was located in the middle of the strip mall with various restaurants and boutiques on either side. The Pot o' Gold dealer had a narrow sign stretching across the entrance. It was a rainbow with a gold coin at one end of the rainbow. The entrance was recessed from the façade of the store and there was a buzzer button with a speaker-microphone next to the door.

Cheryl, Alan and Marlyse waited in the car while Shane went to the shop by himself. They all thought it would be better for Shane to go by himself rather than a group of four. It would show that he might be naïve about coins if he was alone. Shane had the cigar box of coins in a heavy canvas shopping bag. He rang the buzzer and waited. Within a few seconds a gray-haired man peered out of the window and the door buzzed open.

"Can't be too careful nowadays," the man said as he held the door open. He was a short man with a full head of grayish white hair, carefully combed and parted on the side. His face was round and his eyes were blue and friendly.

"What can I do for you young man?

"I've got some coins I need appraised. Do you do appraisals?"

"I do. But there is a charge if we don't do any business in the way of me buying some of what you have. Come on over to the counter and let's see what you got."

Shane followed the man over to the glass jewelry-store-like counter. It was a long narrow store with a narrow aisle between the counters leading back to a door that had a "Private" sign on it. Shane noticed a man in a fatigue jacket, toward the end of the store where a STAMPS sign was hanging over a small counter.

"My name is Eddie. What's yours son?"

"Shane."

Eddie opened the cigar box that Shane set on the counter. He took out the spreadsheet, looked at it and took out the photos.

"Looks like you did a pretty good job here Shane. Is this list accurate and up to date?"

"As best as I could. I think it is complete and accurate. Some of the coins, like the old quarters had their dates worn and it was hard to determine what the exact dates were."

"That's okay. They're probably not worth anything anyway." As he was talking, he was sorting through the coins and occasionally picking up a coin and looking at it through a magnifying glass on a goose neck stand. His medical ID bracelet was clinking on the glass display-case top. He picked up the 1861-D on the edges with his thumb and index finger, gave it a good look under the glass and carefully placed it back in the box.

As this was going on, the man in the fatigue jacket wandered over next to Shane. Shane glanced over and the man nodded. Shane noticed a bright yellow patch on the shoulder of the jacket with a silhouette of a horse. The man had long mullet style hair hanging over his collar and a full scraggly beard. Shane moved slightly to his left.

"What's he got here Eddie? Anything interesting?"

"Don't know yet, till I do some research"

"Do you mind Son?" The man said as he picked up the 1861-D and gave it a long look on both sides. "Where'd you get this son?"

"They were my grandfather's. Just want to see what they're worth."

"You got any more of them gold ones there?"

"Back off and give us some privacy," Eddie said giving the man a stern gaze and grabbing the gold coin from the man's hand. The man moved slowly across the aisle.

"Don't mind him Shane. He likes to hang around here. Never buys anything. He thinks he knows a lot about coins. He knows a little. Enough to be dangerous. So . . . here's what I'll do. You leave all this with me and I'll do some research and see if you have anything of value here. I don't usually buy the run of the mill collections left by someone's father or grandfather, but if I find something that I can purchase and sell at a profit then maybe we can deal. How does that sound Shane?"

"Sounds good. How long will it take?"

"I should be done in a week or so. I see you have your name and phone number on the list. I'll give you a call when I'm done. I have to ask the same thing that he asked," Eddie said as he swiveled his head and nodded toward the man. "Do you have any other coins? The gold one in particular. Those usually aren't lone riders. They usually travel in packs."

"That's it," Shane said and grabbed a business card showing the same rainbow and gold coin as the sign out front. 'Eddie Symack, Owner - Numismatist — Philatelist'. Shane slid into his shirt pocket.

"Okay then. See you in about a week," Eddie said.

Shane walked back to the car with a smile on his face. He jumped into the back seat next to Marlyse.

They both reached over at the same time and held hands. The thrill of the search of the coin and the search of their emotions was warm and fulfilling. Cheryl, Alan and Marlyse all said together. "Well, what did he say?"

"Easy! Nothing for now. He needs to do some research. But he did show particular interest in the gold dollar . . . along with a creepy customer hanging out there. He'll let me know in a week or two. Can we stop for lunch somewhere? Are you okay to go eat now Mom?"

"Yes. I'm hungry also. There's a Potbelly around the corner. I've got a taste for barbecue . . . that okay with everyone?"

They all agreed and all were happy to see Cheryl was feeling well enough to eat.

11

The following week was to be a week of waiting and trying to keep occupied while waiting for a call from Eddie. Shane planned some fishing and invited Marlyse and Denny. Denny declined but Marlyse gladly accepted. She was never interested much in fishing but it seems that lately she wanted to learn all about fishing with Shane. Shane planned the fishing on days that there was no baseball practice so he kept a pretty full schedule. News about the gold coin slipped into the back of his mind.

The fishing outings were joined with trips to Orchard Island and small picnics. Shane taught Marlyse how to make a Texas rig with a plastic worm in order to keep the hook from snagging the weeds. She was a fast learner and in one lesson she was rigging her own. He taught her how to use the spin cast reels and then a spinning reel; again, she learned easily enough. Bait cast reel teaching would have to wait. Shane was still working on mastering this most difficult of all rod and reel combos for himself.

After they returned from one of their fishing trips Alan and Cheryl were on their deck and greeted them as they walked up to the deck. Both Alan and Cheryl were taking great pleasure in the obvious bond that was developing between Shane and Marlyse.

"How's the fishing going kids?" Alan shouted as they approached the deck.

"Pretty good. Marlyse is becoming a great fish-ermmm. . .err fisherwoman. She's got more patience than me and certainly more than her brother."

"Are you guys planning anything for tomorrow? I have a favor to ask." Alan asked.

"Nothing definite. What can we do?"

"I need you to go with your mother tomorrow for her blood test. Her blood platelets have been running low and they have to monitor them for safe chemo infusions. I have to be out of town for the day."

"Sure Dad. No problem. I can't drive you know . . . no license! But I could drive in an emergency. Remember you did give me some lessons in the church parking lot a couple of times."

"I'm okay to drive Shane. I just need someone with me just in case. You can bring Marlyse if you want," Cheryl offered.

"Up to you Shane if you want," Marlyse said.

"Okay, if you want to come, I'd be happy. What time tomorrow Mom?"

"Anytime. I don't have an appointment for blood draws. It's first come – first serve. Why don't you come over for breakfast Marlyse and we can leave after that? Okay?"

"Okay Mom. Sounds like a plan." Both Shane and Marlyse felt good that they could help out . . . even a little!

After breakfast the next morning they drove to the University of Michigan Cancer Center. Cheryl checked in at the desk where all the blood tests were administered while Shane and Marlyse sat in the waiting area. Cheryl came back after talking to the nurse on duty.

"They want me to go up to the infusion area to get my blood drawn. They said it's a little more sophisticated blood draw than the regular blood count. Shane, get a wheel chair. I feel a little tired."

Shane got a wheel chair and maneuvered their way up to the infusion suite.

Shane parked the wheel chair next to a row of seats and they waited for Cheryl's name to be called. It wasn't long before her regular infusion nurse, Betty, came out and greeted them.

"And who are you, young lady?"

"She's a friend of mine. Along for the ride. Marlyse

this is Betty, Mom's nurse."

"Nice to meet you Marlyse. What a pretty name to go with a pretty girl," Betty said with a knowing look at Shane. Marlyse blushed.

Betty led them into the infusion area and to an empty lounge chair. She explained that after she drew the blood, they would have to wait for the results in case there was anything further they might need to address. The blood was drawn and Cheryl said, "Shane go get me an orange juice please, and get something for yourself and Marlyse. Show her where the coffee room is."

Shane and Marlyse walked over to the coffee room. Shane grabbed one of the huge Einstein onion bagels out of the warming cabinet and asked Marlyse if she wanted one. She declined and took a sherbet out of the refrigerator. As Shane was spreading cream cheese on his bagel, Betty came into the room for a coffee. Shane looked at his bagel and at Marlyse's sherbet and he thought of Chrissy.

"Betty. Can I call you Betty?" Betty nodded. "Do you remember a little girl I talked to here – the last time I brought my mother here? She wore a *Little Mermaid* scarf. How is she doing?"

Betty's eyes welled up. She was tough from all the sad things she witnessed on a daily basis, but this hit her heart like she was punched.

"Oh Shane, I'm so sorry. She passed away. She was such a brave and pretty girl with her *Little Mermaid* scarf and panties. She never complained. Never said 'why me?' You jogged my memory from your last visit. Chrissy told us that a nice man gave her a sherbet when she couldn't find an ice cream. Do you remember that Shane?"

Shane couldn't speak as he pinched his neck and choked down the tears and felt his heart beating in his chest. He just nodded at Betty. Marlyse could see the emotion on both Betty and Shane. Betty put down her coffee and gave Shane a warm hug. Shane grabbed an orange juice and they started back to the infusion suite. Shane was wiping his eyes as they walked.

Betty came back with the CBC (complete blood count) blood test results a short while later.

"Cheryl, the tests tell us that your blood platelets are dangerously low. Normal count is between 150,000 and 400,000. Yours are just a little above the 50,000 mark. So . . . what this means is that we will have to test you before you get your next infusion. We won't be able to give you another dose of Cisplatin if your platelets are too low. You might have to skip a treatment. I must tell you that if they remain low you might need a blood or platelet transfusion or maybe

Dr. Roberts will prescribe a drug to help the situation. I will contact him with the results and let you know what he says. Check your UM patient portal for any messages. Okay? In the meantime, get your rest and I'll give you a list of food you should eat to help build up the platelets.

They all left feeling somber!

The next day Shane got up early and wandered down to the kitchen to get a bowl of cereal. Cheryl, who was usually an early riser, was still in bed. Shane was missing the friendly morning kibitzing with his mother. This was just another one of the changes in their lives that was putting a damper on the family treasures they had . . . and the one they found. He finished his cereal and went back upstairs and tapped lightly on his mother's bedroom door.

"Mom, are you up? Can I get you anything? How about breakfast in bed? I can make some scrambled eggs . . . my specialty."

"I'm up Shane," Cheryl opened the door a crack. "I was just getting dressed. I'll be down in a moment and we can talk over breakfast."

Shane made scrambled eggs and toasted bagels. Cheryl sat at the table and sipped on a glass of orange juice and instant coffee. Their conversation was stunted

. . . not the kibitzing they so much enjoyed. Shane was afraid to bring up his mother's health. Cheryl was afraid of showing her weakness and the worry that burdened her family and most every waking moments.

As they finished and Shane was putting the dishes in the dishwasher, he pushed the conversation from the mundane back to where they enjoyed talking to each other. "Mom, let's see your hair. You said it was coming in curly. Let's see."

Cheryl was a bit startled by Shane's request but smiled as she thought it was a good way to attack the elephant in the room — cancer! She slid back her scarf from her head and removed it. She stood up and slowly turned around to show the back of her head.

"Wow Mom! You weren't kidding . . . I like. A little longer and you'll have to hang up the scarf. I don't know about you but I'm liking the short hair. Less to worry about and . . . Marlyse likes it."

Cheryl smiled. "You two make a great pair and I'm enjoying seeing your friendship grow . . . and be careful . . . don't move too fast." She smiled and Shane smiled back. "Shane, you may not realize it but that relationship and the finding of those coins has really . . . and I mean really . . . helped me getting through this cancer bullshit. I saw a pin at the hospital gift shop I think I'm going to buy it says "CANCER SUCKS." Shane laughed.

'I like. Get a handful. I want one. It'll show we can beat it." Shane put his arms around Cheryl and rubbed his hand over her hair. They both felt a little better after facing the problem head on.

12

Eddie saw the familiar yellow First Army patch on the Ring doorbell screen, hesitated, sighed and finally buzzed him in. He was busy evaluating the cigar box of coins that Shane had left with him.

"How's it going Eddie? Did you find out if that 1861-D is authentic and what it's worth?"

"Yeah, I did. It is authentic and it's worth a few bucks. The problem is that there's a small defect . . . hardly noticeable near the wreath engraving. Why do you ask? You want to buy it?" Eddie said sarcastically.

"Just asking. I did a little research at the library and if it's like you says it is than it's worth more than a few bucks . . . like $30,000. And . . . there is probably more out there based on stories floating around," the man in the fatigue jacket said.

"It's only worth what you can get for it," Eddie shot back.

"Eddie, I'd like that kid's name and address if you don't mind. I'd like to pay him a visit and see if he has more coins. I have a feeling that he's holding out on us."

"What do you mean – us? And no, I won't give you his name or address. That's confidential. My customers are my business. Why don't you open up your own business if you want to buy and sell coins? All you do is hang around her and harass my customers. I wish you would find someone else to bother," Eddie snapped as he looked sternly into the man's eyes.

The man leaned over the counter and got within a hand's-width of Eddie's face. Eddie could smell the booze and the cigarette breath. "You're going to give me that kid's info whether you like it or not, Eddie. If you don't, I'm going to take it – and that won't be pleasant for you."

Eddie was feeling the threat and he could feel his heart pounding in his chest. He tried to yell back at the threat but all he could do was open his mouth as he felt the angina squeezing and tightening in his chest. He knew he had to get to his nitro-glycerin pills. He kept the pills in screw-off pill-cylinder on his keychain. The key chain was hanging on a hook in the desk-alcove behind him. He half turned, holding his chest, gasping for breath and trying to ask for help. He could feel the aching moving up his arm further into his chest. Half-words were coming out of his mouth as the man just stared at him with an evil grin on his face.

Eddie took a lunge for the key ring. He caught one of the keys and as he did, he fell forward pulling the key ring and wall-hook with him. He fell face forward and the pain stopped as everything went black.

The man stepped over Eddie's silent body and looked under the glass coin counter. What he was looking for was on a shelf under the counter. He opened the cigar box and shuffled through the dull silver coins. Eddie had placed the 1861-D in a plastic protective coin capsule. He ignored the photos of the coins and placed the prize coin in his soiled weathered Levi coin pocket. He looked at the Excel spreadsheet and scrolled his eyes down to the bottom of the page and saw the name . . . Shane Krieger – 248-555-1103.

As he turned to leave, he saw the video screen showing the entrance to the shop. He keyed in the event list, swiped the entire list, selected all . . . and hit DELETE!

Cheryl was a bit disappointed with the platelet count being so low but it did explain her lack of energy. She was checking her U of M patient portal every day to see if there was any message from Dr. Roberts or Nurse Betty. The only thing she could see was that her next infusion appointment was still on for the following week. She would follow the diet suggestions for low platelets Betty gave her and hope for the best. She did not want to miss any infusions and have her schedule set back. Her hair was growing back and that was an encouraging sign . . . so she concentrated on that and her family.

Shane and Alan were also disappointed with the blood results so they encouraged Cheryl in subtle ways. They tried not to interrupt their daily family routine wherever possible. Alan went back to work every day, except on her bad days or when he had to take Cheryl for an infusion or a doctor appointment. Shane tried to keep up his summer routines so as not to emphasize the change in their lives. He attended baseball practice – the games would be starting shortly. He fished when there was a chance and he was spending more and more time with Marlyse . . . which he knew his mother approved and – enjoyed – as much as he did!

Cheryl, Shane and Marlyse were sitting on the deck enjoying the summer heat. Cheryl was working on a crossword puzzle; her favorite way to pass time and take her mind of her health. Shane and Marlyse were busy getting their fishing tackle ready for a short fishing trip. Not too far – in case Cheryl needed them.

"Have you heard from the coin guy yet? I'm kind of anxious to find out about the coin as I'm sure the both of you are," Cheryl asked.

"No, we haven't. We're getting kind of antsy also. We might call him later or if you or Dad could give us a lift down there to see what's going on."

Cheryl did not fail to notice the 'We' and 'Us' when Shane answered her. "I can give you a lift down there whenever. I'm feeling a little stronger. I'm going to take Betty's dietary advice. Your father is stopping at Kroger after work to get as much as he can of pumpkin juice, spinach, gooseberries, beetroot, sesame oil, and vitamin C tablets. Sounds pretty delicious huh? If you're Popeye . . . I guess. Oh well – I'll tough it out – if it'll help me." Both Shane and Marlyse wrinkled their noses at the sounds of pumpkin juice and spinach.

"Mom we're going to take a little fishing trip. We won't be long. Marlyse stole a bass plug form Denny's tackle box and she wants to try it out. Do you need anything before we go? We've got our phones with us in case you need anything."

"No, I'm fine. Go and have some fun. I'm working on a *New York Times* crossword so I'll be busy for a while."

Shane and Marlyse grabbed some water, their phones, Shane's tackle box and three rods and loaded the boat and headed for Orchard Island.

Cheryl watched them row out of sight with a much-needed smile on her face and in her heart.

Cheryl was engrossed and making pretty good leeway on the crossword. She felt a cool gust of wind sneaking up on her that ruffled her puzzle on the clipboard she used for her puzzles. She glanced at her watch and saw that she had been working on the puzzle for over an hour and a half and Shane, and Marlyse had been gone that long. As she felt another cool breeze that cut into the hot humid air, she looked up at the sky and saw a bluish-black sky on its way to Lake Bilasaana. She picked up her phone and called Shane.

"You guys had better head back. Have you looked up at the sky? It doesn't look good. You don't want to get caught out there in a lightning storm."

"We're on our way Mom. Should be there in fifteen minutes"

Cheryl put down the phone and her puzzle. She cranked down the umbrellas, threw the lawn chair cushions in the house, cleared off the table . . . and waited for Shane and Marlyse to return. She kept looking at her watch. It had only been five minutes since she called Shane but it felt like an hour. At last, she saw the tiny boat approaching from across the lake, at the same time she saw the dark cloud at the base of thunderheads snap out its first spider web of lightning with a roar of thunder almost at the same time. The closeness of the lightening and the thunder, she knew, meant the storm was close at hand and she was getting worried.

As she sat on the deck chair with her fingers laced and touching her lips, she saw the boat ram into the dock – full force! Shane and Marlyse jumped out of the boat, grabbed their phones and whatever else they could and ran toward the house. They made it just before a clap of thunder made them all jump. They were all safely inside the house and looking out as the wind pushed whitecaps across the lake. Shane had failed to secure the boat strong enough and the wind carried the boat up and half-way out of the water onto the shore.

Shane was standing between his mother and Marlyse. Each holding one of his hands. They were silent. The wind was howling. Tree branches were sweeping across the roof and leaves were being stripped from the trees and sailing around in small eddies every which way.

It was a violent and short-lived storm that left a strong smell of ozone in the calm moist air. When it passed Shane went onto the deck to upright the chairs and the umbrellas that had blown over – taking the tables with them. There was no serious damage, but he saw that he would be busy picking up the debris on the lawn for a while. Cheryl and Marlyse came back out onto the deck after Shane got the furniture set up. They each had a towel and started to wipe down all of the chairs and the tables.

"Looks like we got lucky. I don't see any damage, I may need some help cleaning up the lawn," Shane said looking at Marlyse and grinning.

Cheryl went inside and got three waters and they all sat on the deck and wondered at what they had just witnessed. As they looked across the lake and the air was warming again, they all noticed it at the same time.

"Look kids, a double rainbow! Oh my God! Isn't it beautiful?" The main rainbow shot out from a copse of birch trees and stretched out across the vista and disappeared into Orchard Island. The smaller, fainter rainbow, like a child of the main rainbow, trailed across the sky following the same path.

"Shane, Marlyse . . . Do you know the meaning of a double rainbow?"

They both shook their heads with "uh-uhs."

"A double rainbow is a sign of transformation and a sign of good luck. Let's hope so,"

Cheryl said as she looked at both Shane and Marlyse.

13

Alan returned from work a little early due to the storm. A good excuse to spend time with Cheryl in their most difficult time since they had married.

"You guys okay?" Alan said poking his head out of the door wall and looking at Cheryl, Shane and Marlyse.

"We're fine. Just a little scary until it blew over . . . and I do mean blow!" Cheryl answered.

"How about Chinese for dinner. You call, Shane, and I'll go pick it up. You want to join us Marlyse?"

Marlyse nodded and Shane went inside to get a menu from Furama's. Alan brought home a Chinese family-style dinner with: wonton and egg drop soup, sweet and sour chicken, almond chicken, gai kow, fried rice and of course – eggrolls and fortune cookies. It was a bonding with the Krieger family and sweeping Marlyse into their hearts. They helped themselves to all the different dinner plates and cracked open the cookies and laughed and shared their generic fortunes.

"Alan. Shane needs a ride down to the coin dealer to see what's going on. It's been over a week and haven't heard anything. Are you working tomorrow?" Cheryl asked.

"As a matter of fact, I was thinking of working from home. Did you call the guy? What's his name?"

"It's Eddie. I'll call when we're done here and see what he can tell me."

They all had full stomachs; Shane and Marlyse volunteered to clean up the plates and take care of the leftovers. Alan and Cheryl enjoyed the meal and watching the children clean up as they forgot about their worries – at least for a while.

After the clean-up Marlyse joined Cheryl and Alan on the deck. She was more comfortable with Shane's parents after spending the last couple weeks in and out of their lives. Shane found the business card for Pot o'Gold and dialed the number. The call went almost directly to voicemail with the message "The mailbox for this account is currently full. Please call later."

"No answer and his voicemail is full. I'll call again tomorrow morning and if it's still full . . . can you drive us down there Dad?"

"Sure, no problem. I'll be home so just let me know."

Shane called Pot o'Gold the next morning after 9 o'clock. He got the same mailbox-full message when he tried to leave a voice mail.

Alan and Cheryl were having breakfast: fried eggs, bacon, hash browns and rye toast. Shane came in the kitchen and told them about the full mailbox.

"Let's finish breakfast and then I'll take you down there and see what's going on. We'll give Mom some quiet time . . . no doctors, no infusions, no pesky husband." Cheryl smiled. "Why don't you have something to eat with us? You want me to make you some eggs?" Alan asked.

"I'm fine I'll just have some cereal."

Alan and Shane talked about Cheryl's health as they drove down to the coin dealers. Both were showing their concern and hopes for the best outcome. Alan parked in a spot a little way down from the entrance. All the spots directly in front of Pot o' Gold were taken and there was a small group of people milling around the entrance.

As Alan and Shane approached the shop Alan asked one of the men in the group "What's going on here? We've been trying to reach the store for a couple days. Is it closed?"

"There's a sign on the front door. You should read it, especially if you had some coins in there," the man pointed at the store and Alan motioned with his head for Shane to follow him.

There was an official looking sign posted inside the window of the door that read:

DUE TO A DEATH IN THE FAMILY
THE STORE WILL BE CLOSED
UNTIL FURTHER NOTICE!
IMPORTANT:
IF YOU HAD ANY COINS YOU DROPPED OFF
RECENTLY AND HAVEN'T RETRIEVED THEM . . .
PLEASE CALL THE PHONE NUMBER LISTED BELOW
248-555-2151 Novi Police Department

The same man that Alan had talked to, came up behind Alan and Shane and said "There's something strange going on here. I hear that the owner died under suspicious circumstances. That's why the police are involved. Did you have any coins here?"

Alan looked at the man. He was a man in his seventies with a ruddy unshaven face and a bulbous nose that hinted at many years of drinking.

"Yes, we did. What's your name?"

"Butch, is just fine."

"Thanks Butch. I guess we'll have to call the police department to see what's going on. See ya."

Alan took out a pen and asked Shane if he had anything to write on. Shane had the business card from the coin shop and handed it to his father. Alan copied down the phone number from the notice.

They walked back to the car and Alan asked Shane if he wanted to call the police or if he wanted him to do it. Shane told his father to call.

Alan did a lot of listening and answered with a few short yeses and nods of the head.

"We have to go down to the Novi Police Station to get this cleared up. Sounds like they might have your coins down there but they want to talk to us . . . and maybe clear up this mystery.

It was a short ride to the Novi Police Station on 10 Mile Road. Alan parked in the visitor's parking space and they entered the station and Alan told the police cadet at the desk that they were there regarding the Pot o' Gold coin shop closing and that he talked on the phone to someone regarding the notice.

The teen-age looking cadet asked them to follow him. He directed them to a small conference/inter-rogation room and told them someone would be there shortly. The Spartan furnished room smelled of coffee and nervous sweat. Within five minutes a plain clothes detective entered the room.

"Gentlemen, I'm Sergeant Phillips." The middle-aged detective had a white-wall Marine haircut, a tight waist, a full chest and arms that strained his shirt that evidenced a religious exercise routine. "And you are the people I talked to on the phone? Right?" He asked in a calm and comforting voice. Alan introduced himself and Shane and they all shook hands.

"Can I get you something to drink?" They declined. "I'll be right back," he said and turned and left the room. He came back holding the Macanudo cigar box with Shane's coins. He put the box on the conference table and opened it and took out the pictures of the coins that Shane and Marlyse had taken.

"Are these your coins Son?"

"They are Sir," Shane looked up at Sergeant Phillips.

"Can you tell me if they're all there? I see you took pictures."

As the sergeant was speaking Shane reached in his back pocket and unfolded the copy of the Excel inventory sheet that he and Marlyse had made. He spread it on the table and looked up at the sergeant.

"I have a copy of the inventory here. I did leave a copy with the pictures when I left the coins for appraisal. Do you have the inventory list I left?" Shane asked.

"Nope, this is all we found. Let's back up a little and let me explain. Mr. Symack . . . Eddie Symack, the owner of the shop was found dead in the shop a few days ago." Alan and Shane's mouths were agape. "It appears that he suffered a heart attack. All that sounds pretty normal but when we investigated the death scene — as we normally would for an un-ordinary death scene — we found that the video recording for the doorbell camera was wiped clean. This made us suspicious about the whole scenario. So, we're talking to as many people as we can that may offer clues as to what happened there. Now, with your list can you tell us if anything is missing?"

Shane removed the pictures from the cigar box and finger-poked around the silver coins and said. "I can tell you right now, without looking at the inventory list that there is a very special coin missing. It's an 1861-D gold dollar. I was looking for Eddie to appraise it and see what it's worth. By his reaction — when I dropped off the coins — we were thinking that it might have some pretty good value."

Alan was listening to Shane explain the whole story and was proud of the way he was handling himself. He didn't have much to offer so he just listened to the conversation going back and forth.

"That's very interesting Shane. That missing gold coin may tie into Mr. Symack's death. Even though it looks like a natural death, there may be extenuating circumstances behind it. Let me see that spread sheet Shane."

Sergeant Phillips spread out the sheet and flattened the creases and looked at the list for a few minutes. "This is another strange thing. If you left a copy like this with this box, we didn't find one. And I see that your name and phone number are on the sheet. Do you have any more coins like the gold one you described, at home or somewhere else?"

"We do have a few more at home in a safe," Alan answered. "Why do you ask?"

"Just trying to cover all the bases. It could be that if someone took that list – and it's not back in the shop where we didn't see it – then someone might be contacting you Shane to buy your other coins. We'll go back to the shop and look around some more to see if the list is there. In the meantime, if you get a call from anyone, don't tell then you talked to us. Just see what they want and then give us a call. Okay?"

"I can do that," Shane answered.

Sergeant Phillips gave a business card to both Alan and Shane and told them he would let them know either way if they find the other copy of the inventory. They shook hands and Alan and Shane headed home with a fascinating and troubling story to tell to Cheryl, Marlyse and Denny.

That evening, Alan and Shane gathered Cheryl, Marlyse, and Denny on the deck overlooking Lake Bilasaana on another calm, warm summer evening. Shane explained to all of them that Mr. Symack . . . Eddie, had passed away from a heart attack in the shop and the shop was closed for the time being. He explained, with his father's input, how they contacted the Novi Police Department and that they had the collection of coins that Shane had dropped off for appraisal and . . . that the gold dollar was missing from the cigar box along with the Excel spread sheet. The silver coins and pictures were still there. But . . . the video on the doorbell camera was deleted which enhanced the police investigation.

"The detective, Sergeant Phillips, said that they were going to go back to the shop and see if they could find the spread sheet and let us know," Alan offered.

"What now?" Denny asked.

"We don't know. I guess we just wait and see what they find. He also told us to be aware that someone might call us since my name and phone number were on the sheet. He thought that whoever took the gold coin might have interest in seeing if we had more. Which we do. But we should be careful and call him if anyone calls us." Shane said.

Questions and suggestions went back and forth for a while. Cheryl and Marlyse brought out some lunch-meat and cheese, bread, drinks and condiments and potato chips and everyone made themselves sandwiches while they discussed the events of the day.

Alan decided to take another day of working at home. There were no business trips planned and no important meetings that he had to attend. He could easily access his VPN account to access his companies secure computer for any follow up on e-mails or other goings-on while he was at home. He was seeing a slight decline in Cheryl's strength lately and he was concerned, especially after the low platelet count on her last blood draw. Her next infusion was scheduled for next week and he didn't want her to miss it.

Mid-morning and the home phone rang. Alan answered. It was Sergeant Phillips. Shane was close at hand and he could hear one side of the conversation.

"What is it Dad? I could tell you were talking to the police. Did they find the spread sheet?"

"Afraid not. Sergeant Phillips said they looked very methodically through the whole shop and didn't find it. He's coming over in a little while. He wants to see what that gold coin looks like and get a picture for their investigation. Why don't you get one out of the safe? I gave you the combo. Remember?"

"I do. Its Mom's birthday . . . 10-21-19-82. Right?"

"Right. And left." Alan nodded with a smile.

Alan welcomed Sergeant Phillips in and they went into the family room. Shane stood up and shook hands with Sergeant Phillips and took a seat on the couch next to his father. Alan offered drinks but Sergeant Phillips declined.

"Do you have a coin handy Shane? I'd like to take a look and take a couple of pictures if you don't mind."

Shane picked up the coin he had set on the coffee table and offered it to Sergeant Philips.

Sergeant Phillips held the coin on the edges with his thumb and forefinger and flipped it looking intently at both sides. "It's a beautiful coin. I don't know much about coins but it sure looks expensive, historical, collectible and all of that. What's the D for? Do have any idea on how much it's worth?"

Shane stood up as if he was going to give a presentation to his class. "The D designates it was minted at a mint in Georgia – The Dahlonega mint. It was a mint that the Confederates took over during the Civil War. They had it until the war was coming to an end in 1865. They closed the mint and attempted to transfer the gold to a safer place. Some got transferred but some got lost or stolen or whatever . . . so this is one of those coins. As far as its value we're not sure that's why we left one with Eddie. But we think they might be quite valuable." Shane was standing as he showed off his knowledge of the coin's history

"Wow! That's quite a history lesson Shane. You sure have done your homework. Do you have a dark cloth I can put this on so I can get a good background for the pictures?" Sergeant Phillips looked up at Shane and over at Alan.

Alan looked around the room and spotted a dark green Michigan State kerchief that Cheryl used occasionally for a headscarf. He gave it to Sergeant Phillips. Sergeant Philips placed the coin on a clear part of the kerchief and took two pictures of either side of the coin. He pulled up the pictures, checked them for clarity, expanded the pics for magnification and nodded his head. "Perfect."

"I assume you have the rest of the coins safely put away. You did say you had a safe? One more thing before I go, Shane. Is there anything else you remember when you dropped off the coins with Eddie? Was there anyone in the shop at the time? Or anything else that was out of the ordinary?"

Now that you ask, I do remember someone in the shop when I was there. Do you want a description?"

"Please."

"He was kind of creepy. An older man with a scraggly beard that nosed his way next to me when I was talking to Eddie."

"How was he dressed or is there anything else that

stood out about him?"

"Yeah! He had on an Army jacket. I don't know what you call it and it had a bright yellow thing on the arm."

"It was probably a fatigue jacket. Did the patch have a line across it and a silhouette of a horse's head?'

"Boy, you are a good detective. That's exactly what it looked like."

"That's an Army patch for the First Army that served in Vietnam. He could be a vet. Was there a name patch over the chest pocket?"

"I think there was but I don't remember what it said."

"Okay guys. I'll get out of your hair now. You've given me a lot to work with. And a word of caution – once more. Be careful of any phone calls regarding the coin and any strangers at the door. We still don't know if that guy has your name and number or some-one else might have it. Keep in touch if anything turns up or if you think of anything else Shane. We'll let you know if anything changes on our end. Thanks again." Sergeant Phillips shook their hands and left.

"I guess we better be careful . . . like the sergeant said," Alan cautioned. Shane nodded his head as he picked up the 1861-D off the scarf and stared at it . . . . wondering?

14

The following week was once again – one of waiting. Shane was waiting for a call from the Novi Police Department regarding the death of Eddie and whether they found his Excel spreadsheet and the marked coin. Alan and Cheryl were anticipating her next infusion appointment and whether her blood platelets had recovered enough for that infusion.

Shane was in the kitchen eating cereal and staring at his laptop screen.

"What's so interesting Shane. You're dripping milk off your spoon on the table." Alan said.

Shane looked away from the screen and down at the table. "Whoops. Sorry. I was just looking up information on how coins are graded. Pretty interesting."

Cheryl came in a few minutes later and walked over to Shane and leaned over and kissed him on the cheek. "Good Morning Son. I see you're wrapped up in your coins again. Anything new?"

"Nope. Just getting info on grading coins. Is your infusion today? I hope things go well." Shane said as he looked up at his mother standing behind him.

"Yes, my infusion is for today. We'll be leaving in a little while. The infusion depends on my platelet count. They'll give me a blood draw when we get there and then . . . we'll wait and wait . . . and hope. Are you going out today?"

"Not for a while. I'm going to go over all this grading information. I'm seeing that there's a lot more to grading a coin than giving it a once over with a magnifying glass. I think Marlyse may come over later to help me understand all this. Dad, would you mind if I call Sergeant Phillips later and see if there's anything going on with the search for that coin we left and the Excel sheet?"

"No. You go right ahead. I'm getting a little impatient myself."

Cheryl and Alan left after a light breakfast of oatmeal and bagels and orange juice. Cheryl brought her crosswords and Alan brought his laptop.

The trip down to the University of Michigan Cancer Center was becoming all too familiar. West on I-96 to South US 23 to M-14 to Downtown Ann Arbor/ Hospital exit, down Main Street to Depot Street, past the Amtrak train station and into the Cancer Patients Only parking garage.

The blood draw was taken at the infusion suite and the wait began. Alan got some bagels and orange juice and coffees while they waited. Cheryl barely bit into the still warm bagel slathered in cream cheese when the infusion nurse Betty came back, holding a sheet of paper. She looked at Alan and then Cheryl.

"Sorry Cheryl. The blood doesn't look strong enough for your infusion today. The count is still well below 50,000."

Alan put his hand on Cheryl's shoulder and hesitated, soaking up the news and trying to feel what Cheryl was feeling. Cheryl placed the bagel on a hospital food tray next to the lounge chair.

"How low is the count and what's next?" Alan asked.

"It's at 30,000. I called Dr. Roberts when I got the results and asked him what we need to do. He said that we have to delay the infusion. We can't take a chance on the Cisplatin reducing the platelets even more. Then we could have additional worries of bleeding and infection. So, he wants you admitted today and for you to get a platelet transfusion. The reason for the overnight stay is that anytime someone gets a transfusion there is concern. And in your case Cheryl, your immune system is compromised so we need to monitor the transfusion . . . and after the transfusion – very closely. I've seen a lot of these transfusions and I've never seen any serious side effects. But we want to be on the safe side. I'll take care of the admission papers. You guys wait here as comfortable as possible and I'll let you know as soon as we get a room for you. Any questions?"

"Not right now," Alan said.

"Will I feel better after the transfusion? I'm really feeling weak and sapped. And I'm putting such a strain on my husband." She looked over at Alan with sad eyes. "And my son Shane."

"I would say yes. You will get some strength and vim back. Not a hundred percent but you will feel better. I'll leave you two and get this paperwork started."

Cheryl relaxed back in the lounge infusion chair and Alan pulled up a visitor's chair and sat beside her so he could hold her hand. Nothing was said but everything was felt. The bagel sat . . . uneaten.

Shane continued researching the grading of coins. He got a handful out of the safe, closed the safe door, but didn't lock it. He didn't want to go through the combination again when he put the coin back.

The gradings were more complicated than he thought when he started his research. He got his goose-neck magnifying glass, he had used for a stamp collection, and set up a high-intensity banker's-light from his father's office on the kitchen table. He began looking at each coin and the nine different grades for Almost Uncirculated coins (AU). There was a separate group of five gradings for uncirculated (Unc) and Mint State (MS), His head was spinning after trying to figure out where his coins fit. *No wonder Eddie was taking so long with the coin collection*, he thought.

He decided to text Marlyse and see if she wanted to come over and help with the grading. She texted him back that she was babysitting and wouldn't be done until after dinner. Just as he gave her a short "K" response his phone lit up with his father's picture.

"Hi dad. What's going on with Mom? Is she going to get her infusion?"

"I'm afraid not Shane. Her platelets are too low . . . and she needs a platelet blood transfusion and she'll have to stay here at the hospital overnight. I'm going to stay here late. I probably won't be home until 9 or 10 tonight. You'll have to fend for yourself. Sorry."

"Don't worry about me Dad. Just take care of Mom and give her a hug for me. Call me if anything changes and I'll see you tonight."

Alan said goodbye and Shane ended the call. Shane pushed the coins aside along with the laptop showing the coin grading information. He grabbed a cold water and went out on to the deck. His attention had shifted to thinking about his mother and father and what they were going through. It was an overcast day and the gray sky blended into the still waters of Lake Bilasaana. He was thinking about all that had transpired over the past few weeks. First was how his relationship had grown with Marlyse and his first kiss with her. Then there was the discovery of the 1861-D gold dollar coin with Denny and then finding the rest of the coins with Marlyse that were buried under the cabin on Orchard Island. The last thing that drastically changed his life was his mother developing cancer. It was a mixed set of fortunes – the wonder of teen-age physical attraction – the joy of discovery of a rare fortune – and the awful feeling of helplessness for his mother.

Shane was lost in all of these thoughts as he sat on the chaise lounge with his elbows on his knees and holding his bottle of water. A figure appeared, walking down the flagstone walkway along the side of the house. Shane caught the movement out of the corner of his eye. As he straightened up and turned his head the first thing that his eyes zeroed in on was a bright yellow shoulder patch!

"Good Morning Shane." The man said as he walked up to the deck and saw the startled look on Shane's face. "You remember me, Shane?"

"Yes. What do you want?" Shane snapped back!

"Just checking in on you and wanted to know if you heard about Eddie. I thought I would follow up and see if you wanted to get rid of the rest of the gold dollars you have like the one you left with Eddie."

"I don't have any other coins . . . and I think you better leave. My dad will be home any minute now. What's your name?" Shane remembered what Sergeant Phillips had asked him about a name tag as he looked at the name patch on the fatigue jacket. It was faded enough that it was just a blur of grey ink.

Shane's bluff was not working on the man. "Never mind my name. Let's go in and see what you've got that I'm interested in. And don't tell me you don't have any more coins. I did my homework and it is highly unlikely that you found just one coin in your grandfather's coin collection. Get up and let's go in-side," The man said as he approached Shane who was still sitting on the chaise lounge with his feet over to one side.

Shane looked up and the man could see the fear in Shane's eyes. Shane had forgotten about all his other thoughts of Marlyse and his mother and was scared into the moment.

The man took out a Buck folding hunter knife and snapped it open. Shane slowly got up with his eyes glued to the knife. The man followed Shane inside and slid the screen door and the main door closed and locked the main door.

It was no use to lie now as the man stared at the few gold coins that Shane had left on the table. They were shining brightly from the banker light he left on. The man walked over to the table and picked up one of the coins and brought it up to his face and turned it slowly.

"I won't hurt you for lying to me. Let's just go and get the rest of the coins and I'll be on my way."

The man was close enough to Shane that he could smell his reeky breath and overwhelming body odor. This added to his fear. He wasn't worried about the coins now – he was worried about his safety.

"Okay, I'll get them. Wait here."

"No, no, no! Not so fast. I'm coming with you. Don't want you pulling a fast one on me."

Shane turned and headed toward the staircase that led up to the master bathroom and remembered that he had left the safe open! As he walked slowly up the staircase, he thought about the gun that his father had shown him in the safe. He needed time to think so he slowed down his pace. The man poked him in the back and told him to hurry it up.

Shane had never even held a gun, let alone how to load a shell by cycling the slide and where the safety was, etc., etc. But he thought, *that didn't matter*. He would have a gun and the man just had a knife. He

walked into the bathroom and looked back at the man still holding the knife.

"Very clever. A safe in the shitter. I see it's even open. How convenient. Now get me the coins. I'm getting impatient," he said poking Shane in the back again.

Because the bathroom was narrow the man had to stand to one side as Shane kneeled down to get into the safe. He was reasonably sure that the man couldn't see into the partially opened safe, as he reached in with sweaty hands and slowly grabbed the gun and stood up.

"Now you can get out of my house," Shane said as he pointed the gun at the man's chest.

The man let out a guffaw. "That gun is not even loaded or cocked. I don't see the red flag. So just give me the gun and get the gold out of the safe."

Shane wasn't sure what the man was talking about with the red flag. He just kept the gun pointed at the man. For whatever reason he thought about watching a Dirty Harry movie with his father and the dialogue just spit out. "Do you feel lucky? Are you sure it's not loaded?" Shane said in a shaky voice and he pointed the gun at the man's groin.

It was now the man's turn to have the look of fear on his face. He stared at Shane. Shane was feeling he had the advantage now and he stared back.

The man – not feeling lucky – turned and walked hurriedly out of the bathroom and down the staircase. Shane followed at a safe distance until the man left through the same door wall they came in through. As he left and disappeared around the corner of the house, Shane still carrying the gun and not thinking about it, raced to the front of the house to see where the man was going. As he got to the front door and looked out the window all he could see was the tail end of a beat-up old black Explorer. He was lucky to catch the Michigan license plate with the "Veteran" designation on it.

Shane looked down at his hand and realized he was still holding the 9mm chrome Kimber pistol. He immediately went into the kitchen and carefully placed the gun on the table next to the gold coins. *What next?* He thought. He picked up his phone and punched in 911.

"What is your name and what is your emergency?" a pleasant female voice asked.

"My name is Shane, Shane Krieger. A man just broke into my house but he's gone now."

"Is anyone hurt? And I need your location."

"No one is hurt. I'm at 4386 Redwood Drive, in Commerce. Can you contact Sergeant Phillips with the Novi Police? He knows all about the person that broke in here."

"I will send a patrol car and have them contact the Novi Police Department. Please stay on the line until the patrol car arrives. Is there anything else you're concerned about?"

"No. Thank you. I do have to call my father but I'll wait until the police get here. I'll stay on the line. Thank you."

Shane put the phone on speaker, laid it on the table, sat down and waited. While he was waiting, he was thinking of what to tell his father. He realized that his father had enough on his plate with his mother going through a transfusion and the status of her cancer treatments on hold. Five minutes seemed like an hour as he heard a knock on the front door. Two uniformed policemen along with Sergeant Phillips were at the door.

"Hi Shane. Are you okay? Tell me what happened," Sergeant Phillips asked as he held the door open for the two Commerce Township police officers to enter.

"It was him. The guy with the army patch from the gold store that I told you about. He wanted to steal the rest of the gold coins that I have," Shane said in a nervous voice.

Sergeant Phillips gave the other two officers the *Readers Digest* version of the backstory on the gold coins. He motioned for them to go into the kitchen so they could sit and Shane could tell the whole story.

Sergeant Phillips noticed the gun on the table, picked it up, pointed it at the door wall, ejected the empty magazine, pulled back the slide to see if there was a bullet in the chamber, let the slide close, and engaged the safety. He had a friendly grin on his face looking at the officers and then over to Shane.

"You scared him off with an empty gun Shane. Good job. Did you know it was unloaded?"

"I have no idea. That's the first time I ever held a gun," he nervously smiled back at Sergeant Phillips and the two officers.

"What else can you tell us about this guy? Did you get a name? Anything else?"

"Couldn't get a name. I tried. His name tag on his Army jacket was faded and I couldn't read it. But I did see his car. It was a beat-up black Explorer. Don't know what year. You know how all the years seem the same. I did see the license plate. It was a Michigan plate and it had "Veteran" on the plate. Will that help?"

One of the police officers was taking notes as the conversation went back and forth. "That will help, Shane. Where are your parents?"

"My dad is with my mom at the hospital. She's getting a blood transfusion . . . chemotherapy."

"Sorry to hear that Shane. Do you want to call your dad and let him know what's going on? You'll have to tell him sooner or later. Best to tell him while I'm here."

"Yeah, your right. I'll call him now."

Shane called his father. Alan answered on the first ring. "Hi Shane. What's going on. Mom just had her transfusion and she's resting and doing okay for now."

"I've got some troubling news. I know you don't need any more on your plate right now but I have to tell you." There was silence on the other end of the phone. "That creepy man that was at the coin shop that I told you about . . . well he broke in here and tried to steal our coins. Sergeant Phillips is here right now. Do you want to talk to him?"

"Are you okay? Yes, let me talk to him."

Sergeant Phillips got on the phone and gave Alan a rundown on what happened and that Shane handled everything the right way and he is okay and the Commerce Police Department would be having a plain police car watching the house for the next couple-three days. He told him he would be available if Alan was coming home shortly otherwise Alan could contact him with any questions. He also told Alan that Shane was able to give them some good information about the suspect's car so they might be able to locate him shortly and arrest him for breaking and entering and possibly more crimes. Sergeant Phillips handed the phone back to Shane.

"Your dad wants to talk to you."

"I'm going to come home and see what's happened and see that you're okay. I need to get Mom some clothes and toilet articles and then I'll head back if you're okay. I'm not going to tell Mom about this just now. She's got to get stronger first."

Sergeant Phillips left and Alan arrived a short while later. He noticed a car with someone in the driver's seat parked across the street and over a couple of houses

Alan gave a rare hug and kiss on the cheek to Shane. "Are you okay? You're probably shook up right now"

"I'm okay now. It was a little scary. Sergeant Phillips made me feel better and the plainclothes cop in the car across the street helps."

As Alan was talking to Shane, he noticed the gun on the table. "What's with the gun out here?"

Shane went through the whole scenario to his father . . . from the time the man approached the house until he was scared off by the gun. He didn't leave out any details. Alan snickered when Shane told him about the Dirty Harry dialogue.

"Are you going to be okay here by yourself while I make a trip back to the hospital? I won't be too long. You could go over to Denny and Marlyse's house if you're concerned."

"I'll be okay Dad. And there's that cop out front if anything happens."

"We'll just have to be careful until the police catch this guy. I hope it's not too long," Alan said.

Alan went up to the bedroom and Shane followed with the Kimber in his hand – a little more comfortable now.

"You better lock this up Dad. And maybe I should get some lessons and practice."

"As soon as things settle down, we'll go to the range for some practice."

Alan grabbed some of Cheryl's clothes and slippers and her travel makeup bag and gave Shane another hug . . . and left.

Shane was continuing with his mixed emotions that he was feeling just before the man interrupted him. But now – he had a couple of new ones – the scary confrontation by a man with a knife – his rush of excitement of holding a gun on him and – actually bluffing him to leave! These new emotions would stay with him for a while.

Shane went out onto the deck to sit and resume his pondering. The deck and the view of the lake was always comforting to him. He never really thought about it that way but now he resumed his deep thoughts from before and once again he was taking pause to think about his life and what was happening to it. He just enjoyed his idyllic life and what it afforded him; a life of school and school friends, of sports and ice cream after wins (or even after loses), a summer of fishing – and even more rewarding – with the boat he refurbished and faired, a loving Mother and Father that had jobs they enjoyed that provided economic freedom, an upper-class worry-free house on a lake – and recently – his discovery of a physical and emotional relationship with Marlyse!

These were some of the things he took for granted and never thought about. But now sitting on the deck and staring over the vista of the lake with Orchard Island in view he started to realize what he had and what was drastically changing. Could all of the pleasures he enjoyed disappear or was it just part of life? Words that his father once told him when he had a devastating loss in Little League. *Life is what gets in the way when you're busy making plans.* Was this life getting in the way of his plans? Was the finding of a treasure of gold coins and his feelings for Marlyse part of the plans? And his mother's cancer and the death of Eddie and the attack by the man to steal the coins . . . were they the part of life that was getting in the way? He had never thought so deeply about life, but now he was forced to. It was at his feet and he had to deal with it. The good and the bad.

15

lan felt a little better now that he knew that there would be a police presence at his house in case the man returned that had attempted to rob Shane. Now he could think about Cheryl and what she was going through. He struggled with dividing his time between Shane and Cheryl. Shane was safe, he thought, and Cheryl needed him at her side.

The transfusion of platelets did not go well. Cheryl developed a fever and chills after the transfusion and she would have to stay in the hospital until the doctors felt she was safe and the platelet transfusion was successful. Dr. Roberts explained to Alan – away from Cheryl – that on rare occasions platelet transfusions are resisted by the body's immune system and destroy the platelets. He emphasized that this was extremely rare but they would err on the side of safety and keep Cheryl under observation until they were sure the transfusion was successful so she could resume her chemo treatments.

Alan was sitting on the visitor chair pulled up close to Cheryl's bedside. He was holding her hand and feeling the coolness emanating from her fingers.

"What's going on Alan? Did you speak with Dr. Roberts? When can I go home?"

"I did talk to him. And he assured me that everything is under control. You have a slight fever and you'll have to stay here a day or two. They want to make sure that everything went okay with the platelet transfusion so you can resume your chemo."

"Crazy as this sounds dear . . . but I'll be glad to resume my treatments and get this over with. Sitting here in the hospital feels like a waste of time. But I'll do what the doctor says. By the way, how is Shane doing? I miss him. Another reason to get out of here."

"He's doing fine. We're lucky we have him. He's so much more mature for his age . . . unlike say . . . Denny. I think that lately he's showing even more maturity." Alan was rubbing Cheryl's hand as he spoke and thinking about what he wasn't telling Cheryl.

The following day Shane was still pondering his life's woes and blessings when the home phone rang.

"Shane, this is Sergeant Phillips. Is your dad home?"

"No, he's at the hospital again. I expect him home

later. Why?"

"I need to talk to you and him. There's been some developments on your case with the man that attempted to rob you. I'd like to talk to you and your father in person and give you the details. Could you have him call me and let me know when you two will be available?'

"Yes. I can do that. Is there anything you can tell me on the phone?"

"All I can say is that we got the guy so you don't have to worry about him anymore. I'd like to give you the whole story in person. It would be easier that way."

"Okay. I'll have him call you when he gets home."

Shane called his father at the hospital and gave him the message. Alan told him he would be home later to freshen up and return to the hospital. He told Shane to call Sergeant Phillips and tell him that 3:00 would be a good time to get him at home.

Alan barely got home when Sergeant Phillips rang the doorbell.

"You look like you had a rough day Mr. Krieger. How's your wife doing?"

"Yeah, it's been a couple of rough days. My wife is doing okay but she has to stay in the hospital a couple of more days." Alan glanced over at Shane and Shane saw the same haggard look on his father's face that Sergeant Phillips noticed. "I'll talk to you later Shane when we're through with what's going on with the police here. So, what's the story Sergeant?"

"Can we sit down somewhere while I explain?" Alan led them into the family room and they all took a seat. Alan and Shane with their hands on their knees in anticipation of what they were waiting to hear.

"We got the guy yesterday. Your description of the vehicle and the veteran's plates helped us to track him down. A patrol car spotted him on a dead-end un-inhabited street. It seems that he's a homeless veteran . . . Vietnam . . . suffering from PTSD. It's really a sad story. I . . . I should say we; police officers try not to get emotionally involved with cases but because so many of our officers are veterans, it's hard not to feel for guys like this."

"What happens now?" Alan interrupted.

"He'll be arraigned on attempted burglary and hopefully he can get some needed help rather than jail-time . . . which would make his plight even worse. You can press charges for whatever the prosecutor comes up with or just let the courts deal with it."

"We just want it to go away," Alan said. "We've got enough on our plates. Right Shane?" Alan gave a warm concerning smile toward Shane as Shane nodded back.

"A couple more facets to the case. There won't be any charges regarding Mr. Eddie Symack's death. He had a bad heart and died from natural causes. Maybe there was some trauma that the Vet brought on but that would be hard to prove. And you won't believe this but the guy's name is . . . are you ready? It's Davy Crockett . . . actual legal name. Not David – but Davy. Can you beat that?"

Both Shane and Alan smiled at this interesting tidbit among all of the dire news.

"I have your coin that Eddie Symack put into a protective coin sleeve. I'll return it to you when the prosecutor okays it. It's evidence right now. I'm not sure if you know or if Mr. Symack ever gave you an appraisal value on the coin but the prosecutor tells me that that particular coin with the D on it is worth somewhere north of $25,000. Did you guys know that?"

Both Alan's and Shane's eyebrows arched in unison. "We had no idea. Did you Shane?" Shane shook his head in disbelief. "We thought they might be worth something but not that much. I guess you've got some college money Son."

"I will try to keep this case confidential. We don't want any newspaper articles about a fortune in coins. That could bring us additional problems. If it does get out, you would be wise to go on TV or in the newspaper and state that the coins have been sold or donated or some other story to keep the bad guys far away."

"Good point Sergeant," Alan said.

They shook hands with smiles on all three faces and Sergeant Phillips said he would get back with them as soon as he had more information about the charges and the release of the coin.

After Sergeant Phillips left Alan asked Shane to sit down so he could update him on Cheryl's condition. Shane showed signs of nervousness for what he was about to hear.

"Your mother has had some side effects from the platelet transfusion. Nothing real serious for now, but they want to keep her in the hospital for a few days so they can monitor her. She's been asking about you so I think it would be a good thing if you came with me tomorrow for a visit. Bring Marlyse if you want. Your mother really likes Marlyse and so do I."

"Are you telling me all the facts. Is she going to be alright?"

"I'm telling you everything Shane. Not holding anything back."

"Okay I'll come tomorrow and I'll ask Marlyse. Did you tell Mom about the whole thing with the man and the coins situation?'

"I didn't. Not something she needs to know right

now. When she gets home, we can both tell her the whole story. That information that Sergeant Phillips gave us regarding the value of the coins could be of some concern. I think we should find another reputable coin dealer and find out how to sell them . . . if you want. That's up to you and Marlyse and Denny. They're your coins. And as soon as we get Mom home, we should take them to the bank and put them in a safe deposit box until you decide what you're going to do with them. At $25,000 per coin . . . 30 coins . . . let's see?" Alan scratched his chin as he was trying to figure out how much the coins might be worth.

"That's $750,000 dollars Dad," Shane quickly figured and gave his dad a victory smile.

"I'll call Sergeant Phillips tomorrow and ask him where they got the value appraisal. Maybe he can steer us to a dealer," Shane said.

After Alan showered and changed clothes, Shane brought out lunchmeat, bread, cheese and condiments. They ate and discussed what they needed to do going forward. Alan would be dedicated to Cheryl and her treatment. Shane would support him wherever he could. They would figure out what to do with the coins . . . later. And they would both work to get their lives back to normal. That wouldn't be easy. There was a new normal looming.

Shortly after Alan left to go back to the hospital Shane called Marlyse and asked her to come over. He told her he had some new information on the coin dealer and some other news she needed to know. He told her they might take a nice quiet boat ride over to Orchard Island.

Marlyse arrived a short while after they ended the phone call. They gave each other a warm hug and a short kiss . . . since no one was around.

"I've got a lot to tell you before we take a boat ride." Marlyse immediately had a worried look on her face.

"It's not all bad. Here it is . . . the good and the bad." Shane updated Marlyse on his mother's condition and asked her to go with him to visit her tomorrow. She readily agreed. Then he told her about the attempted robbery. Her elbows were on her knees with her hands on her cheeks and her mouth agape.

"Oh my God Shane! Are you okay?"

He immediately told her that the guy, Davy Crockett, was captured and everything was fine. At the sound of the name Davy Crockett the look on Marlyse's face melted from fear into a bright smile.

"Okay let's go for a boat ride over to the island." Shane said, knowing he had more he wanted to tell Marlyse.

They grabbed their phones and two bottles of water and went down to the dock and got into the boat. The sun was low on the horizon and was painting the surface of the lake a smear of gold and blue. As Shane rowed, he stared at Marlyse sitting on the transom-seat of the boat. She stared back and gave him signals with her fingers if he veered off course toward the island.

Their warm stares connected somewhere in between them and added to the peace and serenity that the lake provided.

They got out of the boat at their personal mooring tree on the small beach and made their way over to the cabin. They held hands even as the path narrowed. They arrived at the flattened cabin and sat down on the log next to the treasure trap door; it was their log now. Shane had his hand across her shoulders as he stared down at the trap door. It seemed so long ago that their adventure had begun. He was struggling to get the right words on what he wanted to tell Marlyse.

"Marlyse, I need to tell you something. Since we started this adventure, I've been getting the warm un-explainable feeling when I'm with you . . . even when I'm not with you and just thinking about you. I don't want to sound corny but I need to tell you. So . . . hear me out. I don't know what love is. I do see it in my parents. How they care for each other. Especially in these difficult times for my mother. I guess maybe that's what love is. Love during the good times is easy. It's the difficult times that show how much you care for someone. We're barely teen-agers and I have this feeling. I don't know? I feel you might have some feelings for me also. Am I right?" He looked directly into her eyes.

"Oh Shane. I do feel that special feeling like you do. And . . . I don't know what it is either. Maybe it's just a close friend sort of thing but I think it's more than that."

They turned directly toward each other and placed their hands on each other's backs and drew close together. Shane's hand drifted down to Marlyse's lower back. Marlyse gently grabbed his hand and placed it on her breast. He left it there feeling the warmth and her heart beating fast in unison with his. Their tongues touched and their embrace tightened.

Enjoying the moment – they both realized at the same time that it was time to stop. They slowly pulled away. They needed to take a breath before things progressed that might ruin this beautiful – warm – emotional – first time – once in a lifetime – feeling! They had found another treasure in the same spot they found the other treasure. This treasure would be much more lasting and meaningful.

16

The following day Marlyse came over and waited while Alan and Shane finished with breakfast, cleaned up the dishes and got ready for a trip to the hospital. In the car Alan prepared both Shane and Marlyse for Cheryl's condition.

"Your mother has been through a lot and she's not looking her usual self, I just wanted to prepare both of you and not to be shocked. She's lost some weight and looking a little tired."

"Thanks Dad. We'll keep that in mind and try not to be surprised. What's her condition and what's the prognosis?" Shane asked.

"Not sure. The transfusion was difficult with side effects and that's why she has to stay these extra days. I'm hoping to talk to Dr. Roberts today and get an update."

Cheryl was sleeping lightly when they arrived and quickly awoke.

"Oh! Hi you guys. Just taking a little cat nap. So glad you came to see me."

Cheryl laboriously scooted up in the bed and smoothed her hair with a weak smile on her face. Shane and Marlyse were a little shocked at Cheryl's appearance even though they had been warned by Alan.

"I know I look like hell. No makeup and trying to grow my hair back. Your hair looks great Shane. I like it short like that. Give me my scarf Alan."

Alan grabbed the scarf from the food tray and helped Cheryl get it on and in place. Shane came close to the bed and leaned over and gave his mother a kiss on her sallow cheek. He could feel the warm remnants of her fever still there.

Cheryl glanced over at Shane and Marlyse standing close to him. She could see the glow on both of their faces and she thought that their friendship was surely evolving into something more. But she knew her son and his maturity and his wisdom beyond his age. She had no fear that they would take a step too far in their relationship.

"Marlyse, I'm so glad you came. Made this visit even better. What are you two up to? What's going on with the coins? Did you get an appraisal from that coin dealer?"

"There's been a bit of a snag with the appraisal and I'm looking for another dealer. No problem. We're in no hurry," Shane said trying to give a positive ring to what could have been a very negative answer.

"Cheryl, I'm going to the nurse's station and see if I can find Dr. Roberts and get an update on your condition. I won't be long. You'll have company while I'm gone."

"Marlyse, maybe you can help me get on some makeup so I won't look so scary and Shane you can go with your father. Us girls will chit-chat."

The nurse's aide at the nurse's station paged Dr. Roberts. Alan and Shane milled around looking at the bulletin board with a cafeteria menu for the week, thank-you notes from previous patients, along with pictures of pets, news for upcoming events such as cancer patient survivors' groups and where to get information on cancer.

It was only a few minutes before Dr. Roberts arrived. He was a tall thin man wearing round wire-rimmed glasses that gave him the appearance of a professor. This was appropriate since he was the head of the oncology department at the University of Michigan and he was a teaching doctor specializing in female oncology. His bedside manner was a bit course. He was a doctor that believed in coming right to the point. He felt that delaying and or trying to soften the blow of bad news often prolonged the agony even more than getting the bad news out first — honestly and bluntly. He approached Alan and shook his hand and offered his hand to Shane. "Shane. Did I get that right?" Dr. Roberts asked.

"Yes doctor. You got it right," Shane responded.

"Cheryl is occupied with a friend of Shane's that he brought with us." Dr. Roberts smiled toward Shane. "I paged you doctor to see what the latest is on Cheryl's health . . . prognosis."

"Let's find a consultation room where we can have some privacy. Do both of you want to hear what the plans are?' Dr. Roberts glanced at Shane.

"Yes. I brought Shane and I want him in on all of the treatments and information that you have. That makes it easier for all of us when there are no secrets. Cheryl likes it that way . . . and so do I!"

They found an empty conference room. It was barely large enough for a small desk and chair and two visitor chairs. There was an in-house UM computer on the desk. When they were all seated Dr. Roberts went right to the prognosis. "I need to keep Cheryl here another day. I know she was hoping to go home today or tomorrow but I need to run a PET scan on her."

Both Alan and Shane looked at each other with inquisitive looks on their faces. "What is a PET Scan?" Alan asked as he leaned his elbows on the desk.

"Without getting into all the technical stuff it's

basically a sophisticated CAT Scan, except it's in color and gives us a lot more detailed information such as blood flow, the body's use of oxygen and sugar and the most important information is how a disease is progressing or better yet . . . in remission. Since Cheryl had to delay her chemo treatments because of the platelet problem I'm concerned that the delay may have allowed the cancer to get another hold on her and possibly metastasized. Sorry to be so blunt but I need to be honest with you. And it could be a good thing if the PET Scan tells us that the treatment is progressing and diminishing the cancer cells."

Both Father and Son were a little shocked. They were hardening their resolve since Cheryl was first diagnosed but this information put a dent into that resolve.

"Are you going to tell Cheryl now about the 'PET Scan or should I tell her?" Alan asked.

"No, no, I'll come with you and tell her. That's my job and responsibility and I'm sure she'll be disappointed and may have questions for me. Shall we go?"

Alan and Shane had trouble keeping up with Dr. Roberts' hurried pace. A trait that he acquired due to his need for urgency in many instances.

"Hello Cheryl. Your husband and son found me. Hello young lady." Cheryl introduced Marlyse to Dr. Roberts.

"We need to talk Cheryl. Maybe just your husband and you for now." Dr. Roberts nodded his head at Alan. Shane and Marlyse got the hint and left the room. They waited outside Cheryl's room. Shane was leaning against the wide wooden patient handrail and Marlyse was facing him. Shane explained what Dr. Roberts had told him and his dad, and that he was worried. Marlyse held his hands and pulled him closer, trying to give him some comfort. They both had moist eyes.

Cheryl took the news of the PET Scan and delay in her release better that Alan or even Dr. Roberts expected. She rationalized that better to check everything out as long as she was in the hospital and to do what they had to. She was trying to be brave in front of Alan and help him be brave for her.

"We'll get you in for the scan as soon as we can. Hopefully today . . . if not then tomorrow morning for sure. And . . . I'll have the results shortly after. Anything else I can do? Any questions? I'm sure they're taking good care of you Cheryl. Got a great bunch of nurses here."

Cheryl nodded. Dr. Roberts turned and left. Alan grabbed Cheryl's hands, leaned over and gave her a kiss on the lips, tasting the saltiness of her tears that started to leak as Dr. Roberts left the room and Shane and Marlyse came back in.

"I'll take you guys home and then I'll come back and have dinner with you Cheryl," Alan said looking at Shane and Marlyse and smiling at Cheryl as he held her hand.

"Okay Dad. Sounds good. Mom, you okay with that?"

"Sure. You guys go and have some fun. Dad and I will have a wonderful romantic candlelight dinner in the hospital cafeteria," Cheryl let out a little giggle, trying to keep her spirits up and trying to help everyone else at the same time.

"I think they're having my favorite in the cafeteria. I saw it on the bulletin board . . . meatloaf and mac and cheese on the side." Cheryl made a huge grimace . . . then smiled. Alan smiled back.

The ride home was quiet; everyone in their own thoughts. Alan freshened up and headed back to the hospital. Shane and Marlyse made some PB&J sandwiches and sipped on lemonade as they ate on the deck. They were feeling a little somber knowing they would have to wait along with Dad and Mom for the outcome of the tests tomorrow.

Alan was working mostly from home lately. The VPN hookup to his company's computer network served him well. He could keep up with all the electronic happenings at the company and his very efficient administrative assistant, Sande, who had been with him since his promotion to Director of Quality, kept him up to date on any items that he needed to address. He attended weekly staff meetings and any other meetings that required his presence. The rest of his waking hours and days were spent with Cheryl and Shane. This was one of those days!

As promised, they went to eat at the UM hospital cafeteria. It was a huge room with ceiling to floor windows looking out onto a climax forest. Very relaxing for the many souls eating there – patients, caregivers and medical personnel. Alan devoured his meatloaf and baked mac and cheese and Cheryl picked at a salad with stir fried chicken.

They went back to her room and spent a quiet evening watching home improvement shows on TV – *Property Brothers* and *Fixer Upper* with Chip and Joanna Gaines. Cheryl drifted off to sleep and Alan gave her a light peck on the cheek and said goodnight. Cheryl moaned and fell back asleep.

It was after 10:00 PM and the hospital was in sleep-mode. Alan's footsteps echoed lightly off the marble floors. His troubling thoughts interlaced with sincere prayers were bouncing off his brain.

The next morning Alan checked his e-mail and saw a notice that there was a message on Cheryl's UM portal. He had her password so he opened it and opened the message center and saw that she had been scheduled for her PET Scan for 8 o'clock that morning. He showered, shaved and grabbed a Toast'em Popup and headed for the hospital. Her room was empty when he got there so he went to the closet-like coffee room near the nurse's station and got a black coffee and headed back to Cheryl's room to wait for her to return.

It was only a short while before Cheryl was wheeled back into the room on a hospital- sized gurney used to transport patients to testing areas. Two attendants helped Cheryl scoot onto her bed. Alan gave her a kiss and asked her how it went.

"Pretty good. I think I slept through most of it. Now that I'm awake I'm really hungry. The techie that administered the PET . . . that's what they call it, said that Dr. Roberts should have results by the end of the morning. You don't have to wait if you have work to do. You can come by this afternoon and we can discuss the results." Cheryl said with a serious look on her face and her fingers crossed on both hands.

"Not a problem. Everything at work is taken care of. I have a great staff and department that are very supportive during this time of need. I'll certainly take care of them at bonus time. I'll have breakfast with you. I'll call the room service and order breakfasts for us. What is your order Madam?" Alan tried to get a smile with a phony French accent as he pulled out a pen and grabbed the paper menu from the tray table. He got a little smile from Cheryl and helped ease the nervous atmosphere.

Shane wandered downstairs shortly after his dad left for the hospital. The Toast'ems were still out so he dropped a couple in the toaster and poured a glass of orange juice as he waited.

Sitting on the deck with his mother and kibitzing was something he missed more each day. It was a lonely feeling. He felt lucky that his relationship with Marlyse was becoming a steady thing and he had someone he could talk to and confide in. His dad was busy for the most part at the hospital or work responsibilities.

As he took his last bite of a Toast'em, Marlyse showed up and gave him a warm smile as she walked up the stairs to the deck. She walked over and gave him a peck on the cheek.

"Any word on the tests yet? I know it's early. I was just wondering."

"My dad just left for the hospital. I'm sure he'll call when he knows something."

"You want to fish or something while we wait. You can take your phone if he calls"

"Yeah, let's fish or just go out on the boat or maybe over to the island. Better than moping around here."

They made their way down to the boat. Shane got in first and held his hand out to help Marlyse into the boat. "Why don't you drive for a change," he said and took a seat on the transom-seat. Marlyse grimaced and took the middle seat. Her rhythm was a bit off at first but she quickly got the hang of dipping the oars efficiently into the water and they moved smoothly across the lake. Halfway to the island she said she was tired and asked him to switch places. He agreed and Marlyse stood up and with hands outstretched to her side she gingerly took a step toward the rear of the boat. It teetered slightly and she fell forward. Shane caught her with both hands at her waist and their faces met. They shared a lingering kiss. And Marlyse's face lit up with an innocent blush.

Shane rowed the rest of the way. They tied up and without thinking they made their way to the cabin.

Sitting on their log near the still covered cellar opening; it was quiet and relaxing with only the occasional crow caw or cardinal whistle.

"You know Marlyse I haven't thought about the coins lately since my mother's problems started, but being here . . . where we found them, I'm wondering again what we should do? What do you think about what we should do?"

"I don't know. I'm like you. I haven't given it much thought lately."

"Since my mother's health went south it kind of took the luster of the coins . . . no pun intended. It's almost as if there was some sort of curse on this so called treasure. Maybe like the King Tut's mummy curse or The Chicago Cubs' goat curse."

"I don't know about curses. I don't believe in them. Don't think that way. Your mother is going to be fine. She's strong. I've been praying for her and so have my parents"

"Yeah, I guess you're right. Just thinking crazy, I guess."

They shared another embrace and kiss and decided it was time to head back and wait for a call from Alan.

17

The test results came back and Dr. Roberts was carefully going over the write-up. He tried as best he could to form common words that would make sense when he explained what the PET scan results told him. Too much technical jargon was usually frightening to a patient and their family. After he finished reviewing the test results, he jotted down a list of the specific items he would discuss with Alan and Cheryl. He decided to eliminate as much of the scary medical words and concentrate on the procedures going forward that would give some light on what could be a dark prognosis. He told his nurse/assistant to call Mr. Krieger and set up a consultation meeting with him and his wife Cheryl as soon as possible. He had been through this many times with other patients but this consult somehow took on a different light. He felt that there was a need to keep the overall test results as positive as possible; as difficult as that might be. His tough straight-forward bedside-manner was softening.

Dr. Roberts' student resident informed him that Mr. Krieger was already in the hospital and they could discuss the results in her room. The resident, Dr. Carolyn Johnston, and Dr. Roberts made their way to Cheryl's room. On the way they discussed the results of the test so that they were both on-the-same-page so as not to present any more drama than they had to, when discussing the test results and the prognosis and treatment going forward.

Alan and Cheryl had just finished their breakfast and Alan was collecting all the dishes, silverware, orange juice cups, a plethora of butter and jelly pods, onto one tray and setting it on the heater cowling near the window for housekeeping to pick up.

As he turned from the window and looked at Cheryl; Dr. Roberts and Resident Johnston were coming into the room. He saw forced smiles on both of their faces and his breakfast seemed to sink a little as did his heart.

"Good morning you two. Just had one of our gourmet breakfasts I see," Dr. Roberts greeted them, trying to lighten the moment. "This is my assistant Dr. Carolyn Johnston. She's a resident here and my main assistant and I have to say she is one of the smartest students I ever had in my classes over at the U." Dr. Johnston showed a brief blush.

Drs. Roberts and Johnston stood shoulder to shoulder next to Cheryl's bed and Alan flanked the opposite side.

"I'm going to get right to the results and please interrupt me if something is not clear or you don't understand some of the jargon I may be using," Dr. Roberts said as he swept his eyes from Cheryl over to Alan.

Alan nodded and Cheryl stared at Alan and then turned her head toward the doctors. She was hiding her nervous hands under the bedsheet, trying not to show her weakness in front of both the doctors, and especially in front of Alan.

"The test results are back. I've reviewed them and discussed them with Dr. Johnston and here they are. I'll try to be as succinct as possible. The scan shows a nodule on your liver Cheryl, and another on your small intestine." Cheryl's face lost what little color it had. Alan reached for Cheryl's hands under the sheet and held them tight. Not only to comfort her but to comfort himself.

Dr. Roberts hesitated a few seconds and then continued with the test results. "That's the bad news. The good news is that we caught these nodules early as a result of the PET scan and we can treat them relatively easily. I'm going to suggest some treatments that I discussed with Dr. Johnston here and she agrees . . .

but the final decision is up to you two. For the nodule on the intestine, I am recommending a re-section of the bowel. The alternative treatment is a colostomy! I don't think you want to consider that, Cheryl, at your young age." He gave her a light rare smile. Cheryl tried to return the smile but she could feel her face numbing up as she forced her lips upward.

"As for the nodule on the liver . . . that can be treated with radiation treatments. Without getting too technical we will be using a proton beam therapy. Since this nodule was caught early it can easily be treated even during your chemo treatment. They'll give you a little tattoo on your belly so they can pinpoint the x-ray."

"Gee, I always wanted a tattoo. Can I get a dragon or a butterfly?" Cheryl interrupted trying to hide her fear and trying to lighten up the room that was growing dark. She was also trying to forget what she just heard . . . *willful ignorance might make the whole thing go away!*

"Did all of that make sense? Do you have any questions?"

Alan asked. "What's a nodule? Is that a tumor? Are they the same?"

"Once again without getting too technical it's usually a growth less than 3 centimeters in size. It can be benign but in your case Cheryl, since you're already being treated for cancer, we have to assume . . . I need to add that I am very encouraged by what I see. I know it sounds dire but with both of the treatments I'm prescribing . . . I'm confident that you can beat this Cheryl."

Both Alan and Cheryl remained quiet – Alan trying to absorb what he heard and Cheryl trying to erase what she heard. Dr. Roberts asked for any more questions and finished with. "I'll leave you two to yourselves and discuss what I just told you. We can schedule the operation for the re-section as soon as you give us the okay. The sooner the better."

Alan looked at Cheryl and she nodded her head – mouthing the word 'okay'. "Okay doctor go ahead and schedule the operation," Alan said. Dr. Roberts shook his head and he and Dr. Johnston turned and left the room.

"I guess we should take the positive aspect that Dr. Roberts gave us about catching things early and treatments that are available," Alan said looking at Cheryll and still holding her hand.

"You're right Dear. I have to try and keep a positive attitude. I'm more worried about Shane now. You have to tell him all that we just heard as soon as you see him tonight. Okay?"

"Okay I will. Not to worry. And . . . he's been handling this pretty good and . . . his relationship with

Marlyse is helping. I think. What do you think?"

"I agree. Maybe you should tell them both at the same time. That might help him. He'll tell her anyway so make it easier on him."

Alan called Shane and told him he would be home early evening and if Marlyse could be there he would fill them both in at the same time. He tried to keep it upbeat and not worry them too much until the evening. The rest of the day in Cheryl's room was a little tense but they leaned on each other emotionally and their strengths ebbed back and forth making a trying episode in their lives a little easier to face!

Shane and Marlyse were patiently waiting for Alan to arrive. They sat in the family room, not paying attention to the muted Fox News on TV. They made small talk in order to ease some of the tension that was in the room. They heard the door from the garage into the kitchen open and they both got up to welcome Alan home. He was wearing a face of tired and worried.

"Hi Dad. Whenever you want to talk. You want to freshen up or something to eat or drink?" Shane said with a slight hesitancy in his voice. Marlyse kept silent and waited for Alan to reply.

"No, I'm good. Let's sit down and I'll go over the whole scenario."

They all went into the family room and Shane and Marlyse sat on the couch and Alan sat on the recliner. He kicked off his shoes as Shane and Marlyse waited for the news on Cheryl.

"I'm going to give you everything I can remember from the doctor's rundown on what happens next." Shane and Marlyse both scooted to the edge of the couch and had their elbows on their knees and their faces in their hands.

Alan decided that he would take the straight forward approach and not to hide anything. He had made some notes when the doctors had left Cheryl's room and Cheryl and drifted off to sleep. He pulled out the notes he jotted down on one of the hospital menus and glanced at it and relayed as much as he remembered and whatever notes jogged his memory for the rest of the prognosis.

As Shane and Marlyse patiently listened, Alan went through the entire premise of Cheryl's medical situation; the platelets, the nodules on her liver and intestine, the need for a re-section operation, radiation treatments, resumption of chemo. It seemed like the list was never ending to Shane and Marlyse . . . and to Alan. They didn't interrupt.

"Well kids, that's it. Any questions?"

They both just stared at Alan and didn't know what to say. Shane finally asked the obvious. "Is Mom going to be okay? You gave us a pretty long list that sound pretty serious."

"I felt the same sense of fear that you guys are feeling right now. But Dr. Roberts sounded pretty optimistic that Mom is strong enough and with modern medicine being what it is and the excellent facilities and doctors at the U . . . he felt that once we're through the operation and the radiation treatments and back on chemo, that Mom can beat this."

Both Marlyse's and Shane's faces showed some sign of easing as Alan relayed Dr. Robert's optimism. "What can we do to help Dad? Anything! We're here for Mom and for you."

"All I can say right now is say some prayers. It can't hurt. And visits to Mom when she's feeling okay for visitors. And I guess the most help right now, since I'll be at the hospital quite a bit − is to take care of the house. We'll do some grocery shopping on the weekend. So, make a list. Go through the pantry and refrigerator and cleaning supplies and see what we need. Marlyse, you can help him. Women have a better sense for this kind of thing. Is that something you can both help me with?" They both nodded. Alan was trying to force his thoughts onto Shane and Marlyse in hopes that they could keep busy and work their way through these troubled times in their lives.

Marlyse was conflicted. She was thinking that if

her and Shane hadn't connected like they had, then she wouldn't be feeling this emotional pain for Shane and his father and now for herself. But as she looked at both Alan and Shane, she was glad that she was feeling the same pain they were. It gave her a closer bond with Shane. And that was a good thing!

18

After the dire news from his father, Shane struggled with the ups and downs of what was happening to his life and the lives of those around him.

There were the down times when Cheryl was going through tough times with operations, radiation and chemotherapy side effects. He leaned on Marlyse during those times and it seemed to help somewhat! And then there were the up times . . . if you could call them that? Cheryl having gone through her operation and was feeling better or completed her radiation treatment or the best part was getting good results from her chemo treatments.

When she would meet with Dr. Hammoud after each chemo infusion, she would get a blood draw and wait for the results. When the results showed a steady decline in her cancer antigen, she would take the test results printout, place a lipstick kiss on the paper and a smiley face, and post it on the refrigerator. These were the days that put an emphasis on how important his mother and his father were to him. Marlyse put an exclamation mark on that emphasis!

It was nearing the end of summer; daylight getting shorter, weather getting cooler, fishing getting better, leaves showing their true colors and Cheryl was getting back to the Cheryl of six months ago. Alan had resumed his daily work routine. Cheryl slowly resumed contact with some of her real estate listings that were being watched by her work associates. Shane and Marlyse resumed their trips to the island on their fishing trips.

It was on one of those trips that the realization of getting back to where they were a few months ago popped to the surface. The cool weather took a day off and an Indian Summer stretch of days brightened everyone's days.

"Let's take a trip over to the island, Marlyse. It may be one of our last while the weather holds. You know Michigan weather. If you don't like it . . . wait a few hours . . . and it will change."

"You're right Shane. I'm all for a trip on this beautiful day."

On the lazy trip over to the island, Shane had a disturbing thought slam into his consciousness. He suddenly remembered that the island would be closing after this season as the Michigan Historic Preservation Network Society prepared the island to become a historic site. That thought knocked another thing that was compartmentalized during his mother's cancer — the gold coins!

They glided up to the usual mooring spot; it had become routine.

Shane stepped over the gunwale of the rowboat and planted his foot into the sand. As he lifted his other foot over the gunwale it caught on the rail and he went face first into the cool water. He lost his breath as his face went underwater and he quickly stood up — completely soaked, shivering with an embarrassing blush on his face. Marlyse stood in the boat, her hands were clasped over her mouth and a steady, loud giggle was pouring through her fingers.

"Pretty funny huh?" Shane said as he looked at Marlyse with a smile. "Give me a hand and get me back in the boat so I can dry off.

Marlyse continued to giggle as she reached over with both hands to help Shane back in the boat. Shane grabbed both of her arms at the elbow and Marlyse did the same. As the giggles continued, Shane gently but firmly pulled Marlyse toward him and into the water.

"How's that for funny," Shane said as Marlyse raised her head out of the water, gasping for air. They looked at each other and giggled together. When the giggling stopped, they realized that the water was warmer than the air so the stooped down into the warm water to catch their breath. They were both wearing shorts and tee shirts and were barefooted. They had brought flip-flops and there was a towel in the boat from a previous trip. There was no hurry to get back in the boat or on the island. They were enjoying the warm water and another moment that would stay with them.

As they knelt on the sand, they embraced each other and kissed. The warmth of their bodies added to the comfort they were enjoying. As their bodies acclimated to the water and started to cool off, they decided to get up on shore and try to dry off in the sunshine. They put on their flip-flops and walked their usual path to the cabin. Shane was having a difficult time trying to keep his eyes off of Marlyse's wet, white tee shirt.

Once they got to '*their log*' next to the cellar door, they were almost dry. They sat down, looked at each other, and started another bout of giggling.

"Okay, that's enough silliness. Let's talk about the coins and what we're going to do with them. Now that my mom is feeling better, I think we should have a meeting with my parents, Denny, and your parents, if you want them part of the decisions."

"I haven't thought much about the coins lately either. So, I guess we need to make some decisions. Having our parents there for some adult input is probably the best way to go. As far as Denny . . . that's another story. He'll probably go along with whatever we decide as long as he gets his cut."

Knowing that this was probably their last trip to the island for a long time, they lingered there until the sunlight was softening and the sun was slipping into the horizon. They talked about what Cheryl had gone through and how their relationship had blossomed and the discovery of the gold coins. They would be starting high school soon so that was another new adventure that they would be facing and they wanted to face it together.

19

They had their meeting with the families the following week. Everyone was there: Shane and Marlyse, Denny and his parents and Cheryl and Alan. Cheryl was excited. This was her first social event since her cancer was officially in remission. They all gathered in the Krieger family room. There were drinks and snacks set out on the wet bar and everyone was seated and waiting for the meeting to start. Mrs. Rashid gave Cheryl a warm hug and told her how well she looked. Cheryl smiled and welcomed the thought.

Alan got the ball rolling. "The kids asked us here for our input on what to do with the coins they found. We did a little research so I'll give you my take on what Cheryl and I found. There are quite a few coin dealers and auction houses available on the internet. It's quite overwhelming if you have no experience in this sort of thing. So . . . here's what I did. I hope you don't mind that I kind of took the presumption and invited a coin dealer slash auctioneer to this meeting. Since we don't know who might be the best to help us, I contacted the Novi Police Department and got the name of the dealer that they used when the coin we left at the Pot O Gold was stolen. I think you all know the story there. Anyway, I invited the manager of the dealer they recommended. It's called Coins of the World. They have a variety of options on how to deal with coins. She should be here shortly. Her name is Diana Apple. Any questions before she gets here?"

Denny's father, Irwin, an older version of Denny, with a barrel shaped body, salt and pepper hair that stuck out on his temples and a ruddy complexion, replied. "So, Alan, that's great that you arranged all this and helped get this off the ground. I guess we should glean all the information we can from this Miss Apple and then help the kids make a decision. Good Job!"

Just as Irwin was finishing up his thanks to Alan, the doorbell rang. Cheryl answered the door and invited Diana Apple in. Cheryl introduced herself and then went around the room and introduced everyone to Miss Apple. She was a middle aged, attractive woman dressed in a navy-blue business suit with a tomato-red silk blouse that accented her short blond hair. She walked around the room and shook hands and repeated everyone's name as she firmly shook their hands.

"Nice to meet all of you and I am excited for all of you, especially you Shane and Denny and Marlyse who found the coins. Alan gave me a little of the history of the find. Our company has been in business since the 1970's. It's a local, privately owned, family business and licensed by the State of Michigan. We're also a member of the Michigan State Numismatic Society.

I'm going to give you a list of options you can take to dispose of the coins and a little of the provenance of the coins that we researched."

Shane raised his hand and asked the question that most were thinking. "What's provenance?"

"Great question Shane. It's a common word used in the coin and antiques business, but not used much elsewhere. It basically means the place of origin and known history and ownership of a coin or any other antique. The police also use it when they have to track a trail of evidence.

"We did our search for provenance based on the coin itself. We didn't want any information from Mr. Krieger so as not to influence our research. So . . . what we discovered in tracing back the history of the 1861-D gold coins is where they were minted and when and by whom. We researched the archives at one of the CSA museums and discovered that a general by the name of Basil Duke was in charge of transferring Confederate gold at the end of the Civil War. In his diary he noted that a wooden box of gold coins and currency was inadvertently left in a boxcar. A Confederate soldier of Northern heritage discovered the box of gold left in the boxcar and turned it over to the General. It was suspected later, when an inventory was made, that some of the gold may have gone missing from that particular box. The soldier was furloughed . . . meaning he was released from the Army, and presumably headed North. His name was lost in history and he was never heard from again. General Duke's diary did not mention his name, only that he was from the North and conscripted to the CSA because he was living in the South at the beginning of the war. There are a lot of anecdotal stories about Confederate gold how it was lost buried stolen, etc. etc. That's about all we could discover about the gold coin provenance until some 150 years later when Shane and Denny and Marlyse continue the provenance. So, Shane, your father told us that you did your own research. How does what I just told you line-up with your research?"

"It's pretty darn close," Shane answered with a bit of pride showing in his voice.

"That's great. Maybe you'll get into the antique provenance business one day." Shane smiled along with Marlyse sitting next to him.

"What I'd like to do now if no one has any questions is give you a run-down on your options in disposing of the coins . . . or not! Everyone comfortable? Need a break?" Everyone shook their heads and sat on the edges of their seats waiting to hear what was next in the saga.

"No questions . . . then here we go. Your options are these: You can sell them individually on eBay – not recommended! You can sell the entire collection to us – recommended. You can put them up for auction at an auction house like DuMouchelles, not bad but you would want a minimum bid option. I'm being perfectly honest that selling to us is the best option. Why? Because we will buy them at 10 percent below appraisal value. We have to make a few bucks . . . or coins, if you will." Everyone smiled. "If you go with the auction sites, eBay or DuMouchelles then you have to worry about all the details and the question of privacy and security. You do not want your names getting out into the public with this kind of money involved. Speaking of money, we had our most experienced appraiser in the area of 19th century gold coins appraise these coins. Alan met us at the bank and let us take the entire collection for a week. All of the coins were rated as very fine. We couldn't find provenance that they were uncirculated, so Gem Uncirculated was the best we could grade them. Except! Except for one coin that has what looks like a metal punch mark near the wreath feature."

Shane looked at Marlyse with a sheepish grin and raised his hand again. "Guilty as charged. Marlyse and I marked the coin before we took it to the coin shop.

We didn't want the coin to be switched or whatever."

"Well, young man, that tap on the coin probably cost you about $10,000 dollars. Oops! One of life's little lessons, I guess, 'Little actions can have large consequences. But, not to worry. The Gem Uncirculated coins are appraised at around $30,000 each. That one coin will be graded as Choice Uncirculated – moderate distracting marks. So, the entire collection of 30 coins is worth around $900,000. We can negotiate later, depending on your decision." Everyone in the room let out an emphatic, "WOW!"

"I think you should let all of this sink in for a week or so. Discuss it amongst yourself and when you come to a decision let me know." As she concluded her presentation, she walked around the room handing out her business card and shaking hands.

Alan stood up as he shook her hand and said. "Thanks for all the great information. I think we have enough to start the ball rolling. We'll get back to you as soon as we . . . I should say the finders, make a decision."

They all got up and Diana Apple left the room of excited, surprised families.

The next day and the following week all the two families talked about was what to do with the coins. They met as separate families and they met together. It was certainly a big monetary decision that none of them had ever made. Buying a new house was probably the only thing that came close to what they were facing. Marlyse met with her family but she also was part of the Krieger family meetings. It seemed like the right thing to do and Marlyse, Shane, Cheryl and Alan all felt comfortable with it.

At the end of the week since they met with Miss Apple, the Kriegers were gathered in the family room.

"Let's invite the Rashid family over and get the final decision on what we're going to do . . . or should I say what you kids are going to do," Alan corrected himself.

"Yeah, I agree. This has been dragging on long enough and Marlyse and I want this to move on," Shane replied.

Denny and his parents arrived a short time later and they gathered in the family room as they did a week ago. Shane stood up, showing his maturity, and spoke to the two families.

"Marlyse and I have been talking separately aside from all the family meetings and we came up with a plan that may interest all of us. We are all in this together, so we should all agree on what to do." He paused, looked at Marlyse and waited for some reaction. Everyone just nodded their heads, signaling him to proceed.

"We think that we should take the deal where we sell the entire collection to Miss Apple and her store. I guess, by what she said at our meeting, that we would probably get the $30,000 per coin, less a ten percent mark down, so that would come up to around $800,000. If we divide it between the families, which sounds equitable, we would each get around $400,000. I can't believe I'm talking about this kind of money. Anyway . . . it is what it is. We also came up with a little side deal that would be strictly voluntary. Each family or individuals would donate around ten percent of their share to a charity. Marlyse and I have decided that we would donate some of the money to the Children's Pediatric Cancer Department at the University of Michigan." This brought a tear to Cheryl's eye as she thought about what she had been through and how Shane reacted when he met Chrissy, the little girl in the coffee room.

"Well, what does everyone think?" Silence. And then Cheryl spoke. "I think you kids have come up with a great plan. The charity plan strikes home. I don't want to sound like a martyr but what we've been through was tough but we got through it and we do — have a lot to be thankful for. So, I'm going to vote yes on the whole plan."

Applause from everyone sealed the deal.

"I'll contact Miss Apple tomorrow and get all the

details about selling directly to her . . . the appraisal value, their take, how the payment would be made, etc. etc. If there's anything any of you want me to ask her, let me know," Alan offered.

Marlyse stood up, cleared her throat and said. "We wanted to see how everyone reacted to the plan and we also have another suggestion that might be very interesting to all of you." She cleared her throat again and nervously continued. "We think that this would be another great adventure to follow this adventure. Mom, Dad, Denny, Mr. and Mrs. Krieger and Shane and myself . . . are you ready? We think we should each take a coin and . . . are you ready? Hide a coin for someone to find their treasure sometime in the future."

There was silence and then smiles broke out on everyone's face, including Denny's.

"Wow! You guys are really creative. I think it's a great idea. We would have to set up some guidelines. I'm all for it." Denny's dad, Irwin, said.

"We have set up some guidelines," Shane answered. "Let's see what you think."

"First of all, each family will get two coins. Mr. and Mrs. Rashid one coin and Denny one coin. Mom and Dad, you will get one coin. Marlyse and I will get the fourth coin." Denny raised his eyebrows when he heard Shane announce him and Marlyse as a team.

He wanted to say something sarcastic but he kept his mouth shut. He didn't want to ruin what was turning out to be a very exciting ending to the treasure saga.

"Once you have the coin you have to hide it in a hard-to-find place . . . but not too hard so no one will ever find it; like burying it in the middle of a forest. You can leave a note with it giving the provenance; a new word I learned." Shane said with a smile and pushing out his chest. Everyone appreciated the comment. "Try to put it in a place that is not heavily visited but would eventually be found. What do you all think so far?"

"This sounds like fun," Mrs. Rashid said. She had been quiet during meeting as she was at the last meeting. She showed her excitement at the thought of being directly involved in a true treasure mystery. She was an avid reader – especially in the mystery genre.

"Any other thoughts on how we should hide the coins?" Shane asked.

"Who's going to know where all the coins are hidden?" Cheryl asked.

"Good point Mom. I guess we should give a contact name with the coin so we know when they're found. And I think we should keep our own coin hiding spots secret; only known to ourselves or our partner.

Denny's mother Camille added, "If you want, I can keep a secret list of who has what and where they hid their coins. I promise I will keep it secret – even from Irwin here. What do you all think?" There was a bit of a silence and then Cheryl answered. "I think that's a great idea Cam. We should have a central spot where all the info is kept. I vote yes." Everyone else raised their hands and said yes in unison.

After a bit more excited discussion, they all agreed on the ground rules and the meeting broke up. The beginning of the end and the epilogue of the 1861-D story was in place. The provenance would continue!

The following day was the beginning of the new normal. Alan had gone back to work. Cheryl was back at the real estate office, now working half days since her strength was returning and Marlyse was babysitting. Shane decided he needed to veg-out and think about everything that happened over the summer that changed – not only his life – but the lives of everyone around him. He grabbed a water – no fishing gear – no phone – and jumped into his boat, the *Cheryl Ann*, and decided to row across the lake one more time on the boat that started this journey through life. The Indian Summer had finished its warming and was leaving for this year. There was a light shower knocking down the dried, dead leaves. They were being propelled across the lake surface by a slight breeze. He rowed as hard as he could, slicing a clear path through the leaves. He worked up a sweat that was dripping down his face and back. He kept up the frantic pace as long as he could and finally parked the oars inside the gunwales and let the boat drift. His thoughts were drifting just as smoothly and quietly as his boat.

His soliloquy of thought started with the boat he was sitting in and how it played such an important role on how the whole summer started and would develop and bring him to this place and time in his young life. What if? . . . What if –his dad had never proposed fairing the old boat of Mr. Sampson? What if – Denny had not lost one of his lures? And what about the Confederate soldier, or whoever, that buried the coins; where was he? Did he drown? Did he make it home? Why did he leave the coins buried? How strange life is! He thought that he was in a good place now. It was a good ending to summer and to all that filled those summer days. Good endings are just that – good. But good endings after overcoming physical and mental adversity are even better! And this ending was better than a good ending. It was overwhelming and sweet and gave Shane a warm feeling when he thought about it. He thought about his mother and the physical and mental pain that she had been through and he thought about his father and himself and what they had to overcome and the support they gave each other and his mother. He thought about his English class and his reading of *A Tale of Two Cities* by Charles Dickens and the opening line "It was the worst of times; it was the best of times." He thought that what everyone concerned had gone through, it was an appropriate phrase to describe the past few months.

His next thoughts were of Marlyse and how their relationship started with the fishing and the discovery of the cabin on Apple Island and the gold coin treasure and the warm emotional and physical feeling that they shared. He realized that this relationship made the fight that his mother faced, that much easier. He knew in his heart that he wanted it to continue his relationship with Marlyse as long as it was in his power and if Marlyse felt the same way. He was afraid it would end! That would not be good! He thought about what his father had told him that *life was what got in the way of the plans we made*. He thought about Eddie Symack dying and the Veteran Davy Crockett suffering from PTSD. The emotion he was feeling was broken as his thoughts drifted back to that day in the hospital when he met Chrissy, The Little Mermaid girl. He wondered about heaven and if Chrissy was up there and looking down on him with a smile and thanking him for thinking about her. He wiped a tear away. He thought about Denny and how their friendship was instrumental in starting his friendship with Marlyse. He thought about the double rainbow that he and his mother and Marlyse saw after the thunderstorm on Lake Bilasaana. How his mother told him and Marlyse that a double rainbow was a sign of transformation and good luck. It certainly was both of those to the nth degree. As his mind-movie drifted with his thoughts he was startled when the boat sent a vibrating thud through his feet as it ran into a log on the shore of the island. It was the same log near the copse of birch trees where they always tied up the boat. It was as if the boat had a spirit-of-its-own and knew where to dock. Shane took the cue and decided to take one last solitary walk to the cabin. His and Marlyse's cabin.

It was a lonely walk without Marlyse there or Denny chattering. The air was calm and quiet. The birds seemed to have been placed on mute for Shane to continue his thoughts. The only sound was the crunching of his footsteps on the newly fallen leaves – the sound of stepping on corn flakes. He walked the familiar path to the cabin and sat on the moist log next to the door to the cellar. He lifted the door and peeked inside to see the broken step on the ladder and the hole where he had dug out the crock with the treasure of gold coins. He got up, left the cabin site, and turned and said loudly, "Goodbye old friend!"

The rain-shower had stopped. There was a smattering of pink cotton candy clouds – and a rainbow

— with a story — on the far horizon of the lake. He got into his boat and started his trip back home to his family — and to Marlyse!

THE END

EPILOGUE

T he good-luck of the rainbow shined for quite a few years.

Alan and Cheryl picked up on their near perfect life after Cheryl's bout with cancer. They both retired after successful careers and spent their twilight years on Lake Bilasaana with yearly exotic vacations.

Shane and Marlyse continued their relationship and their discovery of love lasted and strengthened as they grew into young adulthood. After high school they attended Michigan State University; living in separate dorms they still managed to see each other on a regular basis. Shane received a BS degree with a major in limnology (the study of lakes). Marlyse received a degree in botany with an emphasis on pomology (the study of fruit and its cultivation). They married shortly after college. Shane was hired by the State of Michigan DNR (Department of Natural Resources). Marlyse worked for Oakland County and was assigned to work with the Historical Society department in care of the Orchard Island restoration. They had their ideal jobs – the last two pieces of life's jigsaw puzzle. The fortune they had found on Orchard Island had faded into their memories but was always peeking back at unexpected times.

They donated a portion of the treasure to a fund at the University of Michigan C.S. Mott Pediatric Oncology department. They contacted Chrissy's parents (the *Little Mermaid* girl that Shane encountered during his mother's infusion visits). They received permission to use Chrissy's image for a mural on a wall that contained a 90-gallon salt water aquarium. A small but efficient ice-cream-room was built next to the aquarium wall and designed to accommodate the young patients; with heights of all the counters and freezer easily accessible. Shane and Marlyse would visit regularly to ensure the maintenance of the aquarium, visit with some of the patients and nurses and make sure that ice cream, sherbet and snacks were plentiful and regularly stocked. It was called "Chrissy's Room".

After a few years of working at their dream jobs, they decided to start a family. Their son Alan, named after his grandfather, grew into a clone of Shane. He married and had a son named Brady, after his great grandfather's favorite quarterback.

This is where the rainbow started to fade!

It was one of those dark, dreary, rainy, cold, December nights. Alan was driving with his wife Catherine in the passenger seat. Baby Brady was sound asleep in his infant-seat in the rear seat. The truck in the opposing lanes shot across the median and hit their car head-on. Alan and Catherine died instantly. Brady was left with just a few bruises.

Baby Brady's future was determined as soon as his parents were killed. He would be raised by his grand-parents, Shane and Marlyse and his great uncle Denny.

Shane and Marlyse moved into Shane's childhood home on Lake Bilasaana after his parents passed away. Alan and Cheryl had lived a long and rewarding life.

After a few years of trying to figure out his fu-ture, Denny decided that with a business degree in his pocket he would look into purchasing a business with his share of the treasure. As luck (that word again) would have it, the Pot o' Gold coin shop be-came available after years of being run by the Symack family. Denny became a certified numismatist and his business thrived. He never married and he also moved into his parent's home after they passed. And so . . . the close-knit neighborhood resumed. Denny took a renewed interest in fishing and spent countless hours with his great nephew Brady. Close to a father-son bond!

On most of their fishing excursions on Lake Bilasaana, Denny would tell his great nephew the story of the treasure of the coins. Brady never got tired of listening to his great uncle tell the story. It seemed as if the story changed with every telling . . . sometimes a little . . . sometimes a lot! On one fishing trip, just before Brady was getting ready to go away to college, Denny told him the story of the coin-hiding agreement between the families.

He told Brady that each member or couple was to hide a coin somewhere where it might be found in the future and the provenance of the coins would continue. He told him that his mother and father (Irwin and Camille) had decided to wrap the coin with a caution note to the finder that the coin was valuable and they dropped it into a Salvation Army kettle at Christmas time. When it was found, the story of the coin received local and national attention.

He told him that his great-grandparents, Alan and Cheryl had decided to hide the coin in the fruit cellar where the original treasure was found. Since their daughter-in-law, Marlyse worked for the historical society on the island she told them that there would be ongoing searches for history on Orchard Island —especially near and around the cabin. She was right! Years after they buried the coin it was found by a team of archeological students from Michigan State University.

The final two coins, he told Brady, had yet to be found. He didn't tell them where they were but did tell him that they were somewhere in or around Lake Bilasaana.

Denny had attached his coin to a fishing plug and carefully lowered it into "The Hole" where it snagged on the underwater tree. He cut the monofilament line he used to lower the plug and left it for some curious soul, like he and Shane were, to find the coin.

The last coin was hidden by Shane and Marlyse in a carefully cut out notch on the bottom of the transom seat of the *Cheryl Ann*.

Shane and Marlyse died within months of each other, holding on to the secret of hiding place for their coin. Denny moved in with Brady at the Krieger home on Lake Bilasaana. The *Cheryl Ann* sat idle, neglected and overturned on the shore. A few months after funerals for his grandparents, Brady was sorting out storage boxes in the garage. He came upon his grandfather's notes on how to fair a boat. He asked his uncle Denny if he knew anything about fairing a boat. This brought a broad smile to Denny's face. He explained the fairing process as he looked at Shane's printout of fairing with handwritten notes made in the margins. They decided to fair the old boat one more time.

Brady recruited one of his friends to help him drag the *Cheryl Ann* into the garage where they turned it up-side down and placed it on the wooden saw-horses that Shane had used for the original fairing. A week into the sanding of the keel, Brady was chiseling out dried up caulking from one of the joints when he heard a metal sound hit the cement floor. He peeked under the boat and saw the gold coin nestled in the sanding dust. He picked it up, carefully and nervously, and raced to show his uncle Denny what he had found.

Denny's sparkling grin matched the glow of the coin. He pulled out his jeweler's loupe, that he routinely kept in his pocket, examined the coin and told Brady that he had discovered the original coin – the one with the pin prick that Shane and Marlyse had marked. Uncle Denny told Brady of the value of the coin which got an exuberant "WOW" from Brady. Money aside . . . he decided to keep the coin that held so much love and history and mystery.

There was only one more coin to be found. The one attached to a lure hanging on the branches of the overturned pine in "The Hole" on Lake Bilasaana. That one would have to wait for an unknown adventurer for the provenance of the 1861-D coins to resume.

The End

Lightning Source UK Ltd.
Milton Keynes UK
UKHW020645310521
384676UK00011B/932